The Acorn Wars

TOM HERNANDEZ

COVER BY RYAN BOYCE
AUTHOR PHOTO BY MEGAN JOHNSTON

ISBN-13: 978-1-7331766-0-6

For Danna and Tony Hernandez

*And all those who choose to love another's child
as their own*

CONTENTS

ALSO BY TOM HERNANDEZ

Chocolate Cows and Purple Cheese, and other tales from the homefront (essays)

Abundance – a collection (poetry)

The Edge of Middle – thoughts from the top of the hill (essays, poetry and short fiction)

INCLUDING TOM HERNANDEZ

Write Where We Are – WriteOn Joliet Inaugural Anthology (2017)

Write Where We Are – WriteOn Joliet Second Annual Anthology (2018)

Cheetah Stories: a collection of short stories, poems and essays based on one silly prompt – a WriteOn Joliet anthology (2019)

Write Where We Are – WriteOn Joliet Third Annual Anthology (coming in 2019)

"It is not flesh and blood, but heart which makes us fathers and sons."

— Friedrich von Schiller

AUTHOR'S NOTE

This book is a work of fiction, but like most such works, the "walls" of the fiction rise from a "foundation" of truth. Together, they produce something more interesting and honest, if not always more attractive. Truth is often painful, but it can also be freeing and healing. I believe this is a universal story of courage, perseverance, commitment and forgiveness. Still, to be clear, these are my truths and fictions. Though they may sting some, I present them with deep admiration, appreciation, affection and respect for those who continue to teach me that "family" isn't defined by names, race or even blood, but rather by love.

ACKNOWLEDGEMENTS

This book took seven years – and a lifetime – to write. It wouldn't have happened without the help of many people.

With that in mind, thank you to my:

...cousin Virginia Luna for saying "yes" to a dream.
...WriteOn Joliet friends for their support, patience, good humor and encouragement.
...mentor Denise Baran-Unland for her incredible talent and commitment, which are both inspiring and a tad scary.
...editor Colleen Robbins for mercilessly minimizing the "head jumping" and passive voice. "Was" and "Were" don't stand a chance when she's in the room.
...fellow writer Allison Rios for her kindness, patience and generous help in addressing my embarrassing lack of technical expertise.
...daughters Emma Williams and Olivia Hernandez, and my granddaughter Riley Jean Williams for being the stars that light my sky.
...and first, last and always, my wife Kellie for everything good in my life.

1

It's bad form to laugh at a dead body. Especially your own father's.

Miles Ayala knew this, yet he laughed loudly as he stared at Michael Ayala's lifeless frame. The body lay half-covered under a sheet on a stainless-steel table in a cramped holding room just off the emergency room at Cross of Christ Hospital, routinely shortened by locals to "The Cross."

"You still owe me lunch." Miles smiled and shook his head.

"Is everything all right sir?" The question came from behind Miles.

"What?" Miles turned toward the voice. He hadn't realized someone had come into the holding room with him. A large black woman in nurse's garb stood a few feet away. A tag on her uniform said "Lynn." He knew from his days as a newspaper reporter that last names were no longer provided for security reasons. Her right eyebrow cocked, she stayed a few feet behind Miles, out of arm's reach and near the door into the larger waiting area. Miles stepped toward her. She crouched a bit and edged toward the door. For a second, he was confused. *What the hell is wrong with her? Why is she acting so strange?* Then he understood. Having spent his share of time in hospital emergency rooms in his years as a journalist, it dawned on him that she was positioning herself between him and the exit just in case he flipped out. He didn't blame her. A man talking to a dead body didn't seem too bad, but you never know. He'd seen people lose control over less. One can never be too careful working in the emergency room, he knew. Death had a way of tightening reason, like a guitar string, until it snapped.

"Oh, I'm sorry," Miles said, raising his hands and smiling, trying to diffuse the tension. "I didn't mean to frighten you. Yes, I'm fine." Another, softer laugh. "This is my dad," Miles said, staring down at his father who was still in his work uniform though his jacket and shirt were open. Only an hour into death, Michael's skin, usually a rich, dark cocoa now appeared chalky, rubbery, wrinkly and pitted. Michael was fifty-one. Not young, but not exactly old either. *In fact, only twenty years old than me.* The thought came from nowhere and startled Miles. "We were supposed to meet today at Berghoff's to celebrate my birthday next week."

"That's nice," Lynn said. Her tone conveyed more professional courtesy than actual concern. "Do you both work downtown?"

"Yes. Well, I mean, we did. He runs security for a private company and I'm the director of communications for a PR firm."

"So, you're from Chicago?"

"No, we both live in the suburbs. My dad was a cop for thirty-one years. He retired about a year ago and took this new job downtown. And I was a newspaper reporter. I started working downtown about six months ago. We'd meet a couple times each month for lunch."

But there won't be any lunch now. Miles stomped the blizzard's melting remnants from his soaked shoes.

"Well, forgive me for asking, and I don't mean any disrespect, but what is funny about you going to lunch with your dad?" An impatient tone and semi-scowl suggested that she might have other, perhaps more important things to do than sit here and try to decipher the mysteries of some suburban wahoo's life story.

Miles raised his eyes to her. "It's funny because he wouldn't have shown up anyway."

Her right eyebrow peaked again.

"You see," Miles said, "my whole life, my dad would tell friends, family, co-workers, anyone, that he'd meet them for coffee, lunch, whatever."

"Well, that's nice."

"Except that he'd never go." Miles' voice rose a little. "People would laugh and tease him about it, thinking it was funny. Personally, I thought it was very rude. Even cruel sometimes. But he had this charm..." A wisp of sarcasm seeped through his wry smile. "Everyone just loved my dad. They never understood that *they* were the joke."

"And his name was Michael?" She flipped the pages of his dad's medical chart that obviously included his name.

She was trying to make polite conversation and push the topic to a less awkward subject, Miles knew. Still, he never passed an opportunity to chat with someone. To connect in any way, even with a person who obviously cared nothing about what he was saying. Miles craved camaraderie and approval like a diabetic craves sugar. Sometimes, he'd hear himself sharing intimate details with total strangers and think, *Too much information.* Yet he couldn't stop himself.

"Right. Michael. Or 'Mikey'. His family always called him Mikey. He was the baby of the family…"

His voice lagged for a second as his memory pulled down the chestnut family tale like the arm in an old jukebox selecting the chosen 45 from the back and plopping it onto the turntable.

"There's this picture of my dad hanging at my great aunt's house from when he was a year old. It's still there, believe it or not. He had long curly hair like a girl, and beautiful brown eyes." Miles chuckled at the image, as vivid now in his mind's eye as if he were standing in his aunt's living room. "I used to tease him: 'You're either the prettiest boy or the ugliest girl I've ever seen!'"

Then, without warning, a wrenching bawl exploded from his gut as if he'd been punched. His head dropped involuntarily like one big tear onto his father's exposed chest.

"I'll give you some privacy." The nurse started to back out of the room.

"No, no…I am so sorry." Miles wiped the tears from his cheeks, surprised and irritated by his own outburst.

14

"I'm not usually emotional. Jesus, I never cry." Another wave of hot tears crashed in. Angry, confused words erupted from between strangled sobs, like lava burbling from a volcanic fissure. "What the hell?" he demanded of his own flailing psyche. "I've seen people die and then had to talk to the families and write about it." Miles struggled to catch his breath. Finally, enough air seeped into his lungs to expel more frustration with his own perceived weakness. "Christ, this is stupid!" Miles choked back tears, trying to regain control, but the rivers continued to flow over his cheeks, soaking his neck and collar.

"Don't apologize," Lynn said. "You have every right to cry. That's your father lying there." A soft, consoling smile framed her practiced, yet sincere words of support. The kind of smile adults give to children who have scraped a knee, designed to hush cries, ease pain and restore order.

"Thank you," Miles said, grateful for her gentle absolution.

But her kindness did little to ease his consternation. Miles remained flustered by his emotional outburst. All these tears after the years of animosity, anger, embarrassment and pain – physical and psychic – that Michael had caused so many, including himself, but most especially Miles' mother? More pain than Miles could excuse or explain. More than anyone not intimately familiar with Michael – the charming clown, the hard-shelled softie – could accept or understand. So much so that Miles asked himself the questions again that he'd posed in his heart many times. *Who is this man, really? Can*

I forgive him for what he's done? Is it enough to simply say, 'He's my father'? And if he is my 'father', then who am I? The potential answers were perhaps even scarier now in his own burgeoning fatherhood than they had been in a lifetime of childhood.

Then, almost as quickly as they'd started, his tears stopped. He felt strangely empty; void of feeling. A cacophony of chaos rose in place of the short-lived quiet. The former reporter in him took over. His dad used to say that good cops were cops all the time, not just when they were on the clock. Reporters were the same way, Miles thought, as he mentally noted the litany of noise: Rattling gurneys. Paramedics shouting orders to nurses. Crashing metal doors. Streams of gangbangers' "Yo-Yo-Yo-ing" obscenities. Emergency radios clicking and squawking. Televisions blaring in the nearby waiting room. Cops chattering with medical staff, taking notes for reports – a few asking nurses for their phone numbers. The poor and homeless begging whatever free help they could get. Babies screeching, trying to explain the pain they did not understand in the only language they had.

Life – jarring, arrogant, sharp, unbowed, brassy, unrelenting, pounding, unsympathetic and most of all, loud – slapped him hard and yanked him back to the reality of the moment. He turned to Nurse Lynn. "Is there a phone I can use? I have to call my mother."

Now the work of death began.

<u>2</u>

Only a couple hours before, Miles had emerged from the subway stairs into the white teeth of a blizzard.

He cautiously raised his eyes to a gray sky. God spat wet snow in his eyes for his trouble. To his right stood the row of blue and yellow and red newspaper vending boxes clinging to the rail of the bridge over the Chicago River. Already running late, Miles only glanced quickly at the headline screaming from behind a layer of icy slush on the clear plastic door: "January 9, 1997: heaviest snow in decades predicted."

He plodded shakily to the curb, waving his arm in the air. "Taxi!" There were few cabs to hear him. One checker-boarded car skated by and skidded perilously around the ice-slickened corner half a block ahead. "I don't blame you pal, I wouldn't stop either." Miles stared up the street. "Ah, shit, what a nightmare. God, I hate winter." Resigning himself to six blocks of frozen hell, Miles lowered his head, squared his shoulders like a linebacker on the prowl for a running back and bulled into the swirling, stinging wall of white agony.

The newspaper headline was right. This was the worst snowstorm Chicago had seen in years. Irritation spread quickly through Miles' short body like the liquid heat from a shot of whiskey. The hunched backs of hundreds of other commuters sheltered him a little from the wind but did little to stop the snow from turning his head of thick brown hair into a salt-and-pepper mop. Wetness crept down his neck despite layers of scarf and coat and sweater.

A few months ago, the chance to work in downtown Chicago in a big public relations firm seemed too good to pass up. He happily jumped in a new direction after ten years as a reporter at a series of suburban daily and weekly newspapers. And what a direction! East! To the City of Broad Shoulders. Like Truth for Truth's Sake, working in Chicago is its own reward. And then of course there are the people, music, culture, and oh yes, the food! Even better, his dad had also just started a new job at a private security firm a few blocks away. Miles remembered telling his father about the new job. Michael seemed equally excited.

"We can get together for lunch, and maybe you can bring the babies with you to work someday so I can show them off to everyone," Michael suggested.

"Sure, if we can swing it. I bet they'd love riding the train. Maybe we can even take them to a White Sox game," Miles agreed.

It would be extremely difficult to bring a toddler and an infant to work. Miles knew too that Michael preferred football over baseball, specifically the Chicago Bears. But they'd finally made a precious connection, only a few years ago. They could finally talk about something that didn't automatically spiral into bitter disagreement, something they agreed on – his two babies, Michael's first grandchildren. And Miles wasn't going to sacrifice even one toehold on the new bridge they'd started to build.

His dad, good to his word in the first few months, treated Miles to lunch almost weekly. Once he even introduced him around to his buddies at his firm.

"This is my oldest son, Miles. He's a newspaper reporter," he said, emphasizing "newspaper reporter" like the words were gilded.

"*Was* a newspaper reporter," Miles gently clarified.

"Now I work for a public relations firm. I help companies plan their marketing strategies, figure out what they're going to say to the media, that kind of thing," Miles would tell his dad's friends. He chafed a bit at their polite, but less-impressed responses. He understood. PR doesn't have quite the sheen of journalism, even among former reporters turned PR guys.

Michael's apparent pride in his membership in the Fourth Estate both amused and confused Miles given their many debates over social issues, philosophy, politics, religion. Like the red and black clamps on a set of jumper cables, he and his dad could peacefully co-exist unless they touched. Then sparks flew. Michael was a hard-core conservative. A hawk anxious to throw anyone and everyone into jail who gave off even a whiff of guilt. And woe to those who actually broke a law. Any law. In Michael's view, the state couldn't power up the electric chair fast enough.

Proving God has a sense of humor, Miles had proudly joined the ACLU. The government's only true role was to guarantee equality for everyone, he'd argue. Dinnertime clashes became the legendary stuff of family lore when Miles was in college – "Where they actually teach and encourage you to *think for yourself*!" he'd scream before storming away.

But today, working in Chicago wasn't such a prize. Today he'd have given ten skyscrapers and twenty cab rides for a pair of dry boots.

He could have sworn he heard Mother Nature – the bitch! – hissing through the swirling torrent, mocking and chastising him: "You should have stayed in the suburbs with your nice warm car, boy! The Big City is no place for the likes of you!"

A battalion of salt-stained shoes churned the compacted snow into a disgusting gray slush. Miles looked for a sign that the snow was slowing. Instead, the sky looked even lower and thicker. Snow lit on his eyelashes. Miles blinked to clear his vision. He hit a slick patch and his right foot shot out. He twisted and felt a bolt of pain in his groin. Groping the air to regain his balance, he finally stumbled into another commuter.

"Hey, watch where you're going! Fucking asshole," shouted the faceless, fur-lined parka with legs.

"Sorry, I slipped. I didn't mean to…" But the Big City clamor swallowed Miles' apology. Not that it would have mattered. The guy didn't hear a word Miles said. Like everyone else, The Parka was in a hurry to get someplace warm.

"Be careful next time," the Parka said, and stomped up the sidewalk. Miles stood still, exhaling steaming clouds. The slushy ocean of people flowed past him like a sliver of ice that had broken away from the main berg. "Goddamn it, I should have just stayed in bed." He should have known that the day would be perilous. Driving – actually, "sliding" – 15 miles to the train, only to stand on a frozen platform for 30 minutes, only for the train to be 30 minutes late getting to the station, and for what? To sit trapped in a half-empty office with the handful of people also too stupid to stay home.

"Aaaarrrgghhhh!" Miles wailed, overcome by frustration. A few people looked his way. None stopped. Even the homeless guy huddled in a doorway just past the bridge a few yards away ignored him and continued begging for coins. "Thank God I'm not dying here!" he yelled. Finally, he tightened his scarf, slammed his gloved hands into the pockets of his overcoat, lowered his face and pushed forward toward his office. *Five miserable blocks to go…*

Miles trudged into his office building's lobby feeling like he'd just climbed Mt. Everest. Soaking wet and trailing puddles, he paused to catch his breath. Despite the morning's disaster, he loved coming here. His mood lightened as he took in every detail of his still-new work home – bright, big and brassy, just like the city itself. Polished steel ribs bracketed twenty stories of sparkling glass panes dividing concrete walls covered by red and blue checkerboard fiberglass panels. A mix of governmental and private offices and public mall lined the exterior of the building. All surrounding a vast, shimmering, airy public vestibule both too hot in the summer and too cold in the winter, ironically because of its very size. Critics frequently made this public-private architectural mish-mosh the butt of a lot of jokes, but like so many things about Chicago Miles found it beautiful despite its flaws.

He drew from its intrinsic energy like one of its thousands of light bulbs and felt better just being a small part of it. Most mornings the twinkling goliath sang with life. Corporate employees. Government officials. Uniformed guards. Members of the military. Tourists. Suburbanites. Homeless. Street musicians. A dozen languages being spoken simultaneously, mixing (not always well) with a dozen different smells. The boisterous buzz of humanity was exhilarating. Flakes of conversation flurried in the air as people powered toward the elevators.

"Isn't it beautiful? Girl, I love the snow…"

"Did you see that accident on…"

"The way the waves crashed and froze along the lakeshore…"

"I took the bus, and this guy was…"

"Oh, my goodness, look at my shoes…"

"I hope they let us go home early today…"

"The wind was crazy out there. Look at my hair!"

Miles merged into line for the bank of elevators designated for the higher floors that housed the private offices. The glass cars danced their computerized choreography, leaping and sinking along exposed rails. A bell dinged; stainless steel doors spread wide. Miles followed about 25 others into the car and took a spot near the front along the side so that he could look down on everyone in the lobby. Those still waiting in line or milling around in the lobby watched the passengers in the cars like middle school students fascinated by the guts of a see-through model of the human anatomy.

"I hate the way they stare at us," a woman complained.

"I know exactly what you mean. I feel like they're looking up my dress or something. I feel like I'm part of a freak show," said another woman.

You could be in a freak show or at least a circus, fat as you are, Miles thought.

"Nah, they can't see anything." Miles smiled, never shy about joining conversations uninvited, figuring his wit was usually worth way more than two cents. "Plus, the higher we go, the smaller they get. Watch! They look like ants."

"Yea? Well, they got enough bugs in this place already!" The women laughed, turned back to each other and kept talking.

Miles looked again at the people below. His spirit lifted with each slowly ascending floor. Unnamed faces below milled, poking in and out of the shops that lined the lobby, grabbing their morning bagel or coffee. Sometimes the old "reporter" kicked in and he'd categorize as many people as possible. "Short black male, striped blue suit, probably a lawyer. Heavy white woman, older, maybe a teacher or nurse."

Rising so high made him feel like a comic book superhero that could grow to enormous size. One minute he was a short, mild-mannered public relations guy in a black overcoat, and the next, he imagined a voice booming, "Look! There he is! Giant Man!"

In his secret world he was indeed a giant, at least in stature if not actual physical size. Superior to everyone. *Look at you Little People. So puny. So tiny...*

Once or twice, he'd even jokingly thought about peeing over the railing from the top floor where his office was. He could imagine the commotion.

"Hey! What the hell is that?"

"Is the roof leaking again?"

"Hey, rain ain't yellow..."

"Look up there! Jesus Christ, someone's pissing! Get out of the way!"

He chuckled out loud, breaking the ride's reverie and eliciting a few discomforted stares and glares. He didn't care. He felt big, riding that elevator, working in that place. He smiled, allowing a wave of private pride, the smallest little brag, to wash over the quietest part of his spirit: "This is what I was made for."

The doorbell announced the car's arrival at its last stop. The car settled into its perch with a gentle bump and an electronic female voice purred, "Twentieth Floor."

Maybe today won't be so bad after all.

<u>3</u>

"Morning Josie!"

Miles exited the elevator and headed toward his company's bubbly middle-aged receptionist, stationed about fifteen feet away in a neon brightened foyer behind a counter than ran the length of the office's entryway. Shoulder-length, wavy brunette hair framed a round face anchored by brown eyes that sparkled over the tiny crow's feet at their corners when she smiled.

"Whew! Glad to see you made it in! You wouldn't believe the nightmare I had getting here," Miles said, winding up to tell his traveler's tale.

"Good morning, Miles." Josie's voice lacked the radiant enthusiasm that usually brightened the office. Time had started to erase Josie's youthful beauty, but her vibrant personality more than made up for whatever physical beauty she lacked. "You're supposed to call home, sweetie."

"Ok, I will when I get settled. Man, I thought I'd

never get here. The train was half an hour late, then..."

"Honey, you need to call home now. Your wife said it was urgent."

"...I walked out of the subway and couldn't see my feet in front of me. God, I can't remember it ever snowing so hard. Then I slipped and stumbled into a guy. We both nearly fell down! I tried to get a cab, but no one was stopping for anything. I feel like I'm lucky to be alive, much less be here."

Josie was usually good for ten minutes of laugh-filled story swapping to start the day. But now, not even a chuckle, much less the booming guffaws that normally overflowed the reception area and flooded the private offices behind her.

"Did she say what it's about?" Miles said, somewhat confused by her odd non-reaction.

"No. She just asked that I tell you immediately when you got here. I hope everything is okay."

"She probably wants me to pick something up from this used bookstore I saw the other day. Maybe I'll swing by after I see my dad today. He's taking me to lunch for my birthday."

Josie offered a half-smile, more a gesture of consolation than congratulations. Miles headed to his cubicle. Suspicious of what awaited him on the other end of the waiting phone call – and slightly annoyed by the prospect that whatever it was would require more work – he dialed.

His wife, Maya, answered on the first ring.

"Josie told me to call you immediately. What's up?" Miles tried to dull the edge of irritation in his voice. Like a well-trained dog, he followed a strict morning routine. Chat with Josie. Unload his briefcase. Turn on the computer. Take his lunch to the breakroom. Hit the washroom to relieve the pent-up pressures from the hour-long ride to work. Then check in with Maya. Any interruption of that pattern felt like a pebble in his shoe.

"What took you so long? I've been waiting for more than an hour." Among the many shining facets of Maya's personality that drew Miles to her – the luminous flame for his proverbial moth – was her even-keeled demeanor in the face of just about any chaos. She modeled rational behavior, the world champion of seeking and finding – heck, sometimes even creating – a silver lining from any cloud. Maya stood as the only person able to calm the many storms of Miles' life (both real, and those only he perceived). So why did she sound anxious, even a bit angry, on the phone now?

"I know, the weather is terrible. It took me forever to get here. I should have just stayed home. You should have seen...."

She abruptly cut him off. "Miles, call your mom. Something's wrong with your dad."

Ah, shit, he thought, frazzled by the prospect of another problem on a morning that should have its own dictionary entry under "Trouble."

"Did she say what it is? You know how she 'dramatizes' everything,"

"I don't know. She sounded more upset than usual, but you know how she is with me. She didn't give any details, just told me to call you. Call me when you can, and please be careful. Love you."

"Me too."

Miles hung up. He drew deep breaths, slowly exhaled, counting slowly to ten with each beat. Best to start any conversation with his mother as calmly as possible. He dialed his parents' home in suburban Jordan, about forty miles southwest of the Loop.

"Mom, what's going on?" Miles said, veiling his annoyance behind a curtain of obligatory parent-child respect. He knew from years of experience to keep his complaints to himself rather than risk incurring his mother's wrath. "Maya said something is wrong with Dad?"

"I don't know," Catherine said. Miles thought her tone of voice oddly flat for something that was supposedly urgent.

"Can you please go over to The Cross? An ambulance took him to the emergency room," Catherine said, just as nonchalantly as before.

"An ambulance? Why…what…Have you called over there?" The volume and pitch of his voice both rose a notch.

"Of course! No one will tell me anything, and I don't want to drive in this weather if I don't have to. Your dad shoveled the driveway this morning, but it's covered again, and the plows haven't even come down our street yet."

"I thought you guys just bought a snow blower. Jeez Mom, you know he shouldn't be shoveling."

"We did…I mean, he did…You know what I mean! Look, I don't have time to argue with you. Just get to the hospital and let me know what's going on and if I need to come up there."

Miles clomped back out into the storm, already drained and aching from the exhausting effort to get to work. Wearily, he raised a gloved hand and hailed the first cab willing to test its brakes.

"Where to?" the cab driver asked curtly.

"The emergency room at Cross of Christ Hospital please," Miles said.

"Uh, I don't know, sir…" the driver hesitated. "This storm is pretty bad. I been slipping and sliding all over the place. I am new to this area and I don't like driving in this weather. You can hardly move out here. Is it serious?"

"What the hell do you mean, 'Is it serious'?" Miles snapped. "Would I ask you to take me to the goddamn hospital in a blizzard if it wasn't serious? Jesus Christ!"

Miles slammed the car door and wedged himself into the corner of the backseat to avoid eye contact and more conversation. Short on temper and shorter on patience, he hated being questioned or challenged. Yet this poor guy wasn't to blame for anything, Miles knew. He'd only made an obvious comment. No need to bite his head off. Only a few hours old and already this day was a disaster. Everything about it rubbed him the wrong way: the inconvenience of the blizzard, the burden of the extra chore, the possibility of missing lunch with his dad. And now the inevitable guilt for his flashpoint temper firing, once again, at an unsuspecting, undeserving target.

Miles lifted his eyes to the rearview mirror. "I'm sorry. It's not your fault. This has been a bad, bad morning. Yes, something is wrong. My dad's in the emergency room."

Empathy softened the driver's glare. "I hope everything is alright," he said, shifting the cab into gear.

"I don't know. I'm supposed to find out and call my mom back."

The cab inched slowly back onto the road, the windshield wipers valiantly fighting a losing battle with Mother Nature.

4

Miles' first recollection of his dad was less an actual memory and more a broken picture pieced together and tucked away in a dark mental closet.

A gauzy image framed by the many re-telling's of the story over the years, dimly lit by a boy's awe for and faith in his father, Miles couldn't separate actual fact from hopeful "truth". No matter. In the end, whatever it was, it survived thirty years of joy and disappointment, hate and love, anxiety and elation, shame and pride.

Now, stuck in the back of the cab, he stared out the window. The falling snow obscured his vision as they made the seemingly interminable ride to the hospital, and the memory returned, thickening the emptiness and gloom fogging Miles' heart.

Miles saw an image of himself sleeping on a green sofa bed with his mother, Catherine, and his infant brother, Parker in their tiny apartment on the east side – the poor side – of Jordan. Suddenly, the darkness erupted into a terrifying cacophony: the doorjamb splintering under a heavy-booted foot. The window exploding from the door. A glass lamp taking wing across the room. Catherine screaming at a man lumbering toward them. The blade of a knife in the man's hand shimmered in the nightlight. More crying, not from Catherine now but from himself and Parker, too.

Thirty years later, Miles couldn't remember any actual words, but knew then that the man and Catherine fought about him and Parker. The man, their biological father, Willie Allen, was gone so much, drinking, carousing and even sometimes working that Miles didn't recognize him in the darkness. "Big Willie"-as ironic a nickname as there ever was, considering he stood just over five feet tall-wore a motorcycle club's black leathers, identifying him as a member of what today might be called a gang. He fancied himself some kind of James Dean "Rebel without a Cause" tough guy. In truth he was nothing more than white trash with aspirations no higher than his next beer and, at that precise moment, seeing his two sons who lay on the bed with his estranged wife.

They fought like this often. The last time, only a week before, prompted her to swear she'd to call the police the next time. That bought Catherine and her boys seven days of peace. A respite from the implied threats of raised fists, and the real bruises when the fists did fly, too real to hide, explain or ignore. But the peace ended as it always did, and it looked like this time, Willie meant to get what he came for.

He blocked their doorway. "Let me see my fuckin' kids or I'll kill all three of you," he seethed through a whiskey slur, breathing hard from violent exertion.

"Please, don't, Willie! Don't hurt the boys. Please!" Catherine stood between him and the babies. Her eyes glistened with terror, urgency and utter determination. She would not let anything, or anyone hurt her babies. Catherine punched and kicked the air between them, aiming at nothing, hitting nothing, hoping just to keep distance between the man and her children. "Stay *away!"*

And she wondered for the thousandth time in her young life how things went so terribly off track? What did she do wrong? Why was she being punished?

Around 2 a.m. on a Wednesday morning, Michael took a call of a domestic disturbance on Jordan's far East Side. He grew up in this area, so he knew it well. But this address stood out for a different reason: it belonged to Catherine's — the young waitress he'd been flirting with and trying to ask out for months, so far unsuccessfully. Michael drove as quickly as the situation dictated and policy allowed, squad lights flashing red and blue. He arrived moments later. A motorcycle lay on its side dumped in the front yard.

The front door hung on its hinges, kicked in. Michael carefully looked inside, heard Catherine and Willie yelling at each other, and saw Catherine in her nightgown, blocking Willie from Miles and Parker who lay on the sofa bed crying, terrified by the noise and commotion. Shards of light glinted off Willie's knife blade.

Michael stepped slowly and deliberately into the apartment's front room.

"Drop the knife, and step over this way." Michael's clear, calm, firm, commanding, authoritative tone made it clear that The Law had arrived and wasn't pleased. Unquestioned and unquestioning. A quick "Yes, sir" is the only appropriate (and smart) response to this tone. However, Willie missed this cue. Combative, drunk and desperately misunderstanding his place in the moment, he responded poorly.

"Fuck you, pig!" Willie snarled. Then, a flare of recognition cut through his drunken stupor. "Hey, I know you! You're the asshole who's sleeping with my wife and trying to steal my kids!"

Michael inched his hand toward his holstered gun. He hoped that the mere suggestion of being shot would be enough to deflate Willie's anger.

"I'm telling you again…put the knife down, and step over here." Michael emphatically pointed to a spot at his feet. His arched left eyebrow made it clear that the time for negotiating had passed.

At this point subjects usually understood that Michael and The Law were one and the same and came quickly to their senses. Those too stupid or drunk to get the message often found themselves on the losing end of a scuffle with a young, fit, trained and armed peace officer. Common sense dictates that this is never a good place to be. That was especially so before "Political Correctness" discouraged the police for using all force necessary to protect and serve.

However, standing in the dark apartment, unsure if Willie had exhausted his reserve of anger and not wanting to endanger Catherine and the boys, Michael added a sincere, "Please."

"I just want to talk to you about what's going on here," Michael said.

"You know what's going on, and I know what's going on." Willie's volume lowered, his tongue dragging the extra weight of too much alcohol. "I want to see my boys, and she won't let me! I have a right to see my sons! And now you're here and you're not going to let me see them either. Well, you can all fuck off and go to hell!"

Michael braced for Willie to lunge at him. Instead, Willie stopped, like an electric motor suddenly unplugged. His right hand faltered, then collapsed to his side. Michael dropped his right foot back a fraction of an inch in case the hand should come back up again to fight, but the knife fell and clattered on the wooden floor. Willie stood frozen in place, teetering. Experience told Michael that the booze or drugs were probably taking full effect. Or it could

*be exhaustion or even fear. Whatever. Circumstances just vastly
improved. No one hurt, nothing broken beyond repair. That's the
best kind of police work, Michael knew.*

*"Ok, good," Michael said, soothingly, trying to gain Willie's
trust and cooperation. "That's much better. Let's go outside and
talk about what's going to happen after tonight, and I'll get you
some help."*

*Michael carefully approached, keeping a wary eye trained on
the knife just in case Willie should try to pick it up. He'd seen
subjects drunker than this guy try stupider things. With the gap
closed between them, Michael kicked the knife away. He clamped
his right hand just above Willie's right wrist and put his left hand
on the back of Willie's neck as if to guide him through the door
and help him navigate the front porch steps.*

*Willie took a step before Michael's left hand closed tightly
around a clump of Willie's greasy, dirty, shoulder-length hair, and
pulled. Hard. Willie's head snapped back. Michael's mouth
settled a fraction of an inch from Willie's right ear. Teeth clenched,
his own eyes now furious slivers of power and authority, Michael
leaned over and whispered so that only Willie could hear.*

*"You come back here again, ever"—he tugged again at the word
'ever', like a drummer cracking the snare rim to highlight a note in
a song—"or touch her or those boys, someone will have to arrest me,
because I will kill you myself." Another firm pull on Willie's hair
confirmed that the promise of painful retribution was as real as the
coming sunrise. He gazed straight into Willie's booze-clouded eyes.
"Do you understand me?"*

*Michael stood five feet, ten inches tall. Bigger than Willie by a
full six inches. Still, it wouldn't have mattered if Willie were an
eight-foot giant. The energy in the room shifted. Michael did not
need to need the typical young cop's "tough guy" braggadocio.*

Criminals (and anyone else who crossed him) recognized a deadly truth in his actions. Like the Host during communion in a Catholic Mass, the faith of fear turned Michael's words into something else. They became fact. As concrete and deadly and absolute as the loaded revolver on his hip.

Willie winced in pain, wisely saying nothing.

"Catherine, are you alright? Are the boys ok?" Michael asked.

"Yes, we're fine. Scared, but we'll live. Thank you." Catherine caught Michael's eye. She stared at him, confused and unsettled as much by what just happened, as by the feelings welling up for him. She wanted so badly to kiss him, but she didn't dare in front of Willie who was, after all, still her husband in the eyes of the law, if not in the heart of reason.

"Ok. I'll be back in a little while to get some information and help you clean up," Michael said.

Thinking about it now, thirty years later, Miles could not be sure what happened when the two men exited. He recalled a clatter. As if someone tripped or fell (or maybe was pushed) down the porch stairs.

It wasn't the first time the police had been called to this address. But it would be the last.

***

The cab stopped at the hospital's Emergency Room entrance. Miles peered over the seat at the meter. Seven dollars and fifty cents. He pulled a ten-dollar bill out of his wallet, but a twinge of residual guilt caught his hand. He swapped the ten for a twenty. "Thanks, keep the change. Sorry again for being a jerk."

"No problem," the driver said. "I understand. This weather can drive anyone a little crazy."

<u>5</u>

A dull knife cut into Miles' lower back. He shifted in the hard, plastic chair, hoping to restore blood flow to his numb backside. "Geez," he muttered, "these sure aren't built for comfort."

"No, I'm sorry, they're not," Nurse Lynn consoled. She'd been a lifesaver as he sat, waited, paced, and waited some more. Her jovial demeanor embodied in shining, black eyes set atop full, high, cocoa-colored cheeks that floated with each of many smiles, had shone through after her initial attempts to make sure he wasn't crazy. No harm, no foul, Miles figured, thankful that she'd helped lighten the morning's darkness. "Can I get you anything though while you're waiting?"

"I don't think anything can really help. But thanks anyway," he said.

They'd struck up a conversation to fill the time about the process for dealing with a dead body. That topic had somehow careened into a philosophical thicket about the spiritual and metaphysical nature of life and death. Now they had stumbled over the proper term for whatever it is that animates bodies.

"Well, what do you call it then? The spirit? The soul? The Force?" Miles stood up and shook his legs.

"The Force? Are you serious with that? I loved 'Star Wars' back in the day. Don't tell me you're a fan, too!" Lynn chuckled and her face lit with the energy of the shared connection.

"Of course, I am. What red blooded American isn't?" He puffed out his chest in mock pride. "Han Solo, Princess Leia, Chewie, R2D2, Luke Skywalker, Darth Vadar. How about when Luke found out that Leia was his sister? Or that Darth Vadar…"

They looked at each other and in unison said, with melodramatic gravitas, "WAS HIS FATHER!" More shared laughter.

"Man, now there were some serious Father-Son issues, huh?" Miles added, silently acknowledging the unspoken irony that skipped across his mind. "Well, no matter what you call it, when it's here, a body has life and shape and purpose. Without it, there's nothing but a big lump of flesh." He looked again over his shoulder at his father's still body, covered by a sheet, only its head exposed, waiting for whatever would come next.

"The Force be with you, dad," Miles said in his best James Earl Jones baritone. He and Nurse Lynn laughed, but the thin blanket of humor couldn't completely cover the twinge of sadness in his voice.

He knew it was silly to be debating such a serious thing so frivolously, but what else could he do but talk?

Friends from Michael's company had agreed to drive Catherine to the hospital from her home in suburban Jordan, forty miles west of the city. Normally the ride took fifty minutes. Maybe an hour and ten. But the blizzard must have frozen traffic. And, apparently, time.

Miles stood up, stretched his back until it cracked with relief and started pacing from one end of the waiting room to the other. He felt like a caged animal looking to escape, yet so long a captive that he wouldn't leave even if the door were wide open. Miles had nowhere to go and nothing to do until Catherine arrived. She had to sign the release forms, hospital waivers and insurance papers as Dad's spouse of thirty years. The man known as Michael Ayala was dead. His spirit gone. Yet for the hospital and insurance companies, death couldn't truly begin until Catherine dotted all the "I's", crossed all the "T's" and properly filed the paperwork.

Miles hated insurance companies. *Talk about cold…Of course, the hospital staff knows what to do with dead bodies. But insurance companies run the world, and we just live in it… God forbid anyone should do anything that doesn't exactly meet the insurance company's approval. Bastards…insurance is greatest scam ever created…they probably won't even pay out on Dad's policy…*

"And so here we stand," Miles muttered.

"Excuse me?" a new voice questioned.

A different nurse now manned the reception desk. Miles didn't see her come on duty through the fog of thought around his head. Thirty-ish. Brunette. A little heavy. Too much blue eye shadow. Medium height. And no smile. They certainly wouldn't be talking about "Star Wars" or much else, probably, any time soon.

"Oh, I'm sorry, I wasn't really talking to you. Just thinking out loud." He chuckled, embarrassed at his faux pas. Now he must really look like the crazy person that Nurse Lynn initially considered him earlier. "I didn't realize the other nurse left. I'm just bored and nervous and don't know what to do with myself. I can't leave until my mom gets here. That's my dad back there" – he nodded toward the holding room – "but I imagine it's going to be a while, what with the weather."

"I am sorry for your loss." Those were the right words for a professional caretaker. Not bored, exactly, or even uncaring, but mechanical. Automatic. Practiced. "You say that's your *father*?"

"Yes." Miles subtly dipped his eyes to check her nametag as he approached the registration counter. Sylvia. Again, no last name. "He was my father. Well…um…I mean…until he died. Now he's…well…I don't know what he is…" He tripped over the words like a runner catching his toe on a piece of gravel, losing control, stumbling, catching an anxious laugh before it escaped. He deliberately stopped. Held his breath. Inhaled. Exhaled. Closed his eyes. Opened them. Then, more slowly, he said, "Yes, that is my dad. The doctor said he had a heart attack at work this morning and collapsed. We were supposed to have lunch today…"

Nurse Sylvia returned her over-painted eyes in mid-explanation to the clipboard on the scuffed Formica check-in counter behind the sliding glass window. She interrupted, without looking up. "I asked only because you don't look like you belong to your father."

"Pardon me?" *What a rude insensitive thing to say.*

"I'm just saying you don't *look* like an Ayala." Her eyes raised from her paperwork, then inspected him face to feet, looking for something to confirm his alleged relationship to the deceased. Not really racist, not exactly accusing, but the words still stung, after all these years.

Miles bundled his emotions to keep them in check as he had a million times in his life. He fell back on the explanation long proffered whenever someone braved social protocol and spoke openly what others only thought privately. "Yea, I hear that all the time. I am adopted. My mom remarried when I was a baby, but he's my dad. I always tell people we're related by background, not by blood. He was going to take me out for lunch today for my birthday which is next week. I'm going to be thirty-one. My dad had a funny way of never showing up though…"

Miles realized she already knew what she needed to know about Michael. The rest, she clearly didn't care about. Still, he continued, if only to hear something other than the random medley of modern medicine: intercom chatter, ambulance sirens, paramedics' radios, doctors' shouted directions, the squeaky scuffle of nurses' rubber-soled shoes.

And loudest of all: the incessant, unforgiving ticking of a wall clock.

Nurse Sylvia abruptly looked past him.

Catherine stormed through the emergency room doors, trailed by another wintry blast. Head thrown back, her mouth a taught, imperious scowl, as if she had been kept waiting instead of being late herself, as she usually was. She hugged Miles quickly. The greeting seemed like afterthought but didn't offend him. She tended to deal with business first. Like himself. And everything was "business" for Catherine. Human matters, like grief, came a distant second.

Miles understood his mother better than just about anyone. He spent a lot of time explaining and defending her boorish behavior to the many people she affronted. Still, overwhelmed by the morning's events, Miles simply couldn't excuse Catherine's melodramatic entrance. He exploded. "What the hell took so long? I have been here alone for more than two hours."

"The roads are terrible." Catherine's flat, factual answer included no hint of an apology. "We're lucky we made it here at all. The highway is a mess and Lake Shore Drive isn't even plowed yet."

She inspected the Emergency Room. "Who do we have to see?"

Miles knew he was not going to win this battle. "I guess Nurse Sylvia over there. But don't you want to see Dad? He's in here." He stepped toward the holding room, but Catherine stopped him.

"First I need to figure out how we're going to get him home. Some of the family already asked about funeral arrangements even before I left the house." Anger and resentment always tinted her voice when she talked about the Ayala family.

" 'Him?' Not 'Michael', or 'Your Dad'?" Knowing the turn this conversation would take if he dared speak his thoughts, Miles decided not to raise a sore subject now.

He'd been in this exact spot many times before –in the precarious middle of the tightrope between his parents.

"I wasn't even off the phone with you before people started calling, demanding information from me, telling me where to have the wake, what funeral home to use, ordering me around like I am some maid instead of his wife. How dare they question me? Who do they think they are?" Catherine sputtered.

As he often did, Miles thought Catherine made a mountain out of a mole hill, because she often did. "Mom, they just want to know…"

"I am his wife!" she shouted.

"Stop yelling!" Miles scanned the room to see if anyone overheard her. Luckily, they were alone. "Come over here and sit down." He tried to lead her to a seat, but she jerked her arm out of his hand.

"I don't want to sit! Do they think I can't plan my own husband's funeral? I'll do whatever the hell I want to do, whether anyone likes it or not. I lived with that man for more than thirty years even though he never loved me. His goddamned family is not going to tell me what to do now!"

"I understand." Miles lowered his voice to a stage whisper, locked eyes with Catherine and gently laid his hands on her shoulders, to calm her. "But please don't say that dad didn't love you. He did. Aren't you even a little sad that he's dead?"

Catherine paused. Looked away. Took several long breaths, working out her answer before committing it to words. Finally, she exhaled and turned back to Miles.

"Sad? Yes, but not because he's dead. I can't tell you

how many times I wished your father would die, Miles," Catherine said bitterly. "You know. Better than anyone. You were there. You know how bad he treated me. How many times he hit me. The terrible things he said, and let his family do and say to me." She started getting loud again. "The only thing that makes me sad right now is that I am going to have to put up with more shit from your father's family. More people acting treating him like he was a god, when he should have been in jail himself for what he did to me!"

Her pain was as real as another person in the room. Still, he couldn't believe his ears.

"So, what? You're happy Dad's dead?" Miles said, stunned by her bilious response.

"No, not happy," Catherine said, nearly shouting now. "But I am sure as hell not going to cry over it. I married that man so you two boys would have a father. You needed a father and he wanted a family. He never loved me, at least not as much as he loved you and Parker."

"Jesus, thirty years of this shit..." Miles rolled his eyes and turned away. The conundrum he'd faced his entire life now held Miles' tongue. His head knew the truth behind her words. Yet his heart reminded him of another, simpler truth: the man who gave him a new name, new family, new life, now laid on a cold, silver, stainless-steel table, dead. While he may have often not always deserved it in life, death demanded a certain amount of respect. Finally, Miles decided to just try to appease his mother and pick up the pieces with her later.

"Mom, I know you've been through a lot already

today, and it's just going to get worse in the next couple days. But this is not the time or place to have that conversation." He carefully, firmly measured his tone to respect her feelings and take back control of the moment. "Let's go talk to the nurse."

Sylvia stood at her station, making notes on patient charts. She must have heard everything. How could she not have, as loud as Catherine was yelling? At least she'd pretended to busy herself with paperwork behind her glass partition. She looked up as Miles took Catherine's arm and gently guided her across the emergency room vestibule to the reception window. "This is my mom, Catherine Ayala. Can you please help her get started with whatever she has to do so we can get going? It's been a long morning for her."

"Certainly," Nurse Sylvia said. She handed Catherine a stack of paperwork and issued directions in the same lifeless tone that conveyed her earlier condolences. Catherine started to fill out the requisite forms. "Mom, I am going to go back to my office, if that's alright. You don't need me here, right?" he said, catching the nurse's eye.

"No," she said curtly, focusing on her busy work.

"Ok then. Thank you for your help." Miles suddenly felt deflated, flattened, empty.

"You are welcome."

"Here's some money for the cab," Catherine said, always the parent, digging through her purse.

"No, that's ok. I want to walk."

"Don't be silly. It's freezing. It's a long walk back. You'll get sick and I don't have time to take care of you, too."

"Mom," Miles said, struggling to contain his exasperation. "First, I am fine. I need some time to clear my head. The walk will help. Second, if I do get sick, I am married. You remember your daughter-in-law? She can take care of me. Thank you, but I just need time to think." He turned toward the door.

"Mr. Ayala?" Nurse Sylvia called.

"What now?" The mere prospect of more drama or work exhausted him. "Yes?"

"Sorry you didn't get your lunch," she said, her eyes and smile both soft with sincerity.

Miles finally returned to his office around 1 p.m. after four exhausting hours at the hospital. The snow stopped falling about six blocks into his walk. Chilled to the bone and numb with confusion and frustration, hunger and fatigue battled over his body like competing armies fighting for the high ground. He slogged into the reception area at his office. A quiet, persistent voice kept whispering that something worse perched on the horizon. *Is it paranoia? Reporter's intuition? Both? Who the hell knows?*

However, there sat Josie, the one shining beacon in this miserably dark day.

"Hey Miles! Is everything ok?"

He leaned a little over her reception desk, too drained for the usual pleasantries.

"My dad died this morning. That's where I've been. At the hospital." He stepped toward his cubicle.

"Oh, Miles! Honey! I am so sorry."

He didn't turn back to acknowledge her sentiments.

"Well, aren't you going to go home?"

He stopped. Fair question…Most people would indeed want to go home, he knew, to the comfort of family and friends. But he didn't. Home threatened a thousand well-intentioned questions and condolences, a dozen re-tellings of the day's events. "No, I think I'll stay here and work a while." Miles managed a weak smile. "I'm an old reporter, you know, so I have to keep to my deadlines. Lots of work to do. Plus, I lost most of the day at the hospital and I feel guilty. You know how us Catholics are about guilt." He managed a frail grin.

The truth was that Miles needed nothing more at that moment than to stop.

Stop thinking.

Stop feeling.

Clear away the chaos of the morning with something emotionally undemanding. Clean. Easy. Familiar.

Something to delay the ache that was starting to spread in his chest.

Something that would lift the hefty burden, for just a little while, of being Michael Ayala's oldest son.

6

The train's gentle rocking and hypnotic clack-clack-clack nudged him toward sleep.

His eyelids struggling under the weight of the day, Miles would have welcomed some rest, but his brain wouldn't allow it. Images – Michael's corpse, Catherine's emergency room meltdown – popped up then disappeared from his mind like hummingbirds flitting, now you see them, now you don't, from flower to flower. Worse yet, his head throbbed from the strain and exhaustion. *What I wouldn't give for some whiskey right now…*

Then, as the day's events faded, his brain veered down a mental sidetrack toward an unknown destination: the future. What would the next several days be like? *Am I supposed to help with the funeral arrangements? I suppose I should, but what do I know about burying someone? Just tell me when to show up and where to stand. What do I have to do at the funeral? I hate funerals! There's probably going to be a million people… All that fake smiling, listening to stupid stories, laughing, hugging strangers…Ah well, I suppose it's the least I can do…*

Just as the bands of tension loosened around his aching brain and he started to doze off, the train pulled fitfully into the station, jolting Miles back to life. "Last stop: Westville!" the conductor yelled, walking down the aisle, popping open the car door and helping passengers step gingerly off the train's metal step onto the snow-crusted platform.

Miles followed the crowd to the parking lot as the silver beast emitted a loud burp of steam and settled into an extended rest before it returned to Chicago.

"Oh honey, I am so very sorry!"

Maya threw her arms around Miles as he wedged himself through the front door into their modest, warm house. Miles stared gratefully into her blue eyes. Deep, mature, sparkling and, most of all, forgiving, those eyes drew him like a mouse to a peanut butter-filled trap thirteen years ago. As with Elizabeth Taylor, age would never dilute the beauty of Maya's eyes. They still captured him now, even as crow's feet started to leave inevitable imprints around their edges. Maya's soft gaze reflected her grace-filled spirit and caring soul. She could soothe the sharpest hurts with just a look. Miles knew. He'd seen it with others. Felt it himself. And loved her most for this, of her many gifts.

"I loved your dad so much. I am really going to miss him, and I feel bad that the kids won't get to know their Grandpa Michael."

Miles gently extricated himself from her hug. Maya and Michael had been very close. He had loved Maya like his own daughter and treated her like a princess – especially since she'd presented him with his first, and then his third grandchildren, both girls.

Removing his heavy overcoat, he tried to breathe through the feeling of claustrophobia slowly encasing him.

"I know, sweetheart…listen, I am sorry, but I just don't feel much like talking about it right now. I don't feel much of anything, actually."

Maya gently combed her fingers through his hair, drawing them down over his cheek and neck until her hand settled on his shoulder. "That's understandable. You've been through a lot today. But…" she paused… "Do I dare ask how your mother was?"

Miles turned his head toward his shoulder and kissed the back of her hand, then nuzzled it with his cheek. God, how he loved any chance to touch her. He cradled his hand around hers, lifted it from his shoulder and entwined their fingers. Five couples joined for life…

"She was as you'd expect," he said without further explanation.

That elicited a knowing laugh from his wife, who'd grown used to her mother-in-law's many moods and behaviors. Like many others in the Ayala family, Maya had found herself in Catherine's line of fire often enough to understand exactly Miles' understated response.

"Well, at the risk of making your head explode, go ahead and tell me about it." She hoped the gentle teasing would help ease the tension as clear on his face as his five-o-clock shadow.

"Not much to tell, actually. I stood around by myself for two hours until she got to the hospital, and then when she did show up, she acted like Dad somehow inconvenienced her by dying. She started screaming and yelling her usual bullshit about the family… luckily, I calmed her down before the nurse on duty called security… although part of me was hoping security would come and maybe take Mom to the psych ward!" Only years of experience decoding his sense of humor assured Maya that Miles was kidding—at least, partly.

"Oh, come on!" Maya chided. "I know she can be loud and difficult, but it couldn't have been that bad, could it?"

"Worse." Miles plodded toward for the kitchen, each dragging step siphoning more of what little energy he had left. Twisting the faucet, he pulled a clean glass from the cupboard, filled it, emptied it, then filled it again.

"Honey, why do you do that?"

"Do what?"

"Wash the glass before you use it."

"Well, you never know what kind of bugs or germs or filthy cooties could have crawled inside there and died."

Miles smiled. Maya did not. "Please don't do that. You know it makes me insane. The glass is perfectly clean," Maya said. "I know you want everything to be just so, but you make me feel like I did something wrong when you do that."

"I'm sorry, I don't mean anything by it. It's just a silly habit, nothing more. It's not like I am anal or anything,"

Miles said.

"Not anal? Really? My goodness Miles, even the dust on your desk is in straight lines – I mean, assuming you even have any dust on your desk," Maya teased.

"You know, you've told that joke a million times and it just keeps getting funnier, all the time," Miles said.

He turned back to the cabinet, pulled down the aspirin bottle, pried off the lid and tapped four pills into his palm.

"Are you alright?" Maya asked.

"I just have a stress headache, why?"

"Because that seems like a lot of medicine for just a headache."

"I'm fine, don't worry about me." He laid the pills in the exact middle of his tongue, filled his mouth with water, lifted his chin, shook his head side to side exactly three times – left, right, left, never more or less – and swallowed. He turned back to the sink, washed out the glass again, dried it and returned it to the cabinet. Maya peered into the cabinet. The glass looked like it hadn't been moved.

The throbbing in his head eased a bit as he recounted the morning's events. "It took me at least ten minutes standing there in the middle of the emergency room to calm her down enough to sign the release papers. Luckily there was no one else around. The blizzard must have slowed down all the usual shootings and stabbings." He rolled his eyes and sneered. "It's a good thing she stopped when she did, or they may have needed another metal table for her."

Maya laughed. "Ok, but that's just your mom. She

always yells."

"Right. But do you know that she never asked to see dad's body? At least not before I left. And we were there for almost an hour together. I mean, I know they had problems, but the man was her husband for more than thirty years. If nothing else she might want to confirm that was actually him lying on the fucking slab before she filed the insurance claim!"

"Ok, sweetheart." Maya walked over and put both arms around his neck, gently guiding his head to her face. He stared at her. She looked every bit the young mother: a little tired, her figure fuller than their dating days, her hair slightly unkempt. Yet he thought, "You are so beautiful to me." He cherished Maya for a myriad of things having nothing to do with physical appearance. The things that have always, and will always, carry over and beyond love's first infatuation. He lowered his chin until their foreheads kissed. "Thank you."

"For what?"

"For being you. I don't know what I would do without you. You are every good thing in my life. You bring sunshine to my darkness. You…"

"Oh, stop!" Maya ordered as the blood rose to her neck. Even now, she still blushed a little at his passionate praise. She lacked his gift for eloquence. Instead, her expression usually took the more practical, grace-shaped forms of forgiveness, empathy and sympathy. "You are obviously very angry and hurt and tired, and you have a right to be. Why don't you go lay down for a couple hours? I'll wake you for dinner."

He quickly raised his head again, pointed his index

finger to the sky. His eyes twinkled as he laughed. "No, that's not true. I know what I would do without you."

"What?"

"I would send a lot of people to outer space." His balled fist threw an uppercut to the chin of an imagined foe. "Bang! Zoom! Right to the moon! Everyone who makes me mad. And that's a lot of people," he said in his best "Jackie Gleason" voice.

Maya chuckled, laid her head on his chest and hugged him again. She loved his edgy wit, yet knew the words were laden with a disconcerting truth that she could neither understand nor relieve.

7

His eyes snapped open.

Damn it…I can't sleep…Why can't I sleep? What time is it?

His hand flopped onto the nightstand and groped for the clock. He pushed the light button. The clock pulsed 7 p.m. *Only seven o'clock…Jesus…*

Miles lay perfectly still, staring into circling darkness. *Why did this happen when he was so young? How will Mom survive financially? Will she finally be happy? Does she even care? Why do I feel so numb?*

Not a very religious person, Miles offered a half-hearted plea he hoped might pass for a prayer. *God, I am so tired…please let me sleep…*

He squeezed his eyelids closed and breathed deeply, trying to slow his racing mind. No luck. Flashing neon sparks jumped and jigged in front of his mind's eye. Jumbled geometric patterns swirled and collided, morphed into globs of rainbows, stretched and pulled and snapped apart, and re-formed into new dancing solar systems. Each wave of mental activity crashed against the back of his eyelids until they couldn't withstand the onslaught anymore.

So much for God…

His feet thudded to the floor. The thick, white socks he habitually wore to bed did little to muffle his rising. Two steps later, Miles twisted the doorknob. The door banged behind him as he thumped down the stairs and trudged heavily back to the living room.

Maya, startled by the shotgun crack of the door, looked up from her book. Miles stared at her through eyes carrying bags of exhaustion. "Sorry, didn't mean to scare you," he said.

"What's wrong?"

"I can't sleep."

"Why not?"

"I don't know. If I knew, I'd be sleeping!" He quickly laughed to smooth the sharp edge of his words. "Maybe it's just too early. I guess I can't sleep any time of the day like him," he said, nodding toward their three-year-old Shih Tzu, Doodles, dozing on his special pillow in the corner, blissful in his canine ignorance.

Maya closed her book and patted the couch next to where she sat. "Come over here," she said, her voice smooth and low.

"Honey, I don't want to fool around."

"Neither do I, silly! Just come over here and be quiet."

Miles sat next to her and nuzzled into the crook of her neck. He closed his eyes and breathed deeply, taking in her smell – lightly perfumed, subtle and understated like everything else about her. She gently stroked his head for several minutes. Her gentle touch soothed some of the anxiety that kept his mind awake when his body so wanted and needed to rest.

Miles loved and admired Maya's maternal nature. Their daughters were still only babies, yet he knew he could not have designed a better mother for his children if God gave him a "Build It Yourself" tool kit. Now, just for this moment – but not for the first time in their relationship – Miles was her "baby", cradled and comforted, protected and safe in her loving arms.

"Did I tell you she wants me to do Dad's eulogy?" Miles mumbled.

"Ok," Maya said.

No response.

"I think that makes sense," she said. "You're the oldest, and you are by far the best public speaker in the family."

Miles knew Maya sometimes purposely tip-toed around his feelings to avoid setting off his touchy temper. He appreciated her efforts at diplomacy yet felt guilty for putting her in such a position. Miles rarely offered a vague opinion about anything. His black-and-white views and brusque candor on most every subject could be both a blessing and a curse, sometimes creating an exhausting emotional roller coaster for both of them. He'd lash out at her for no reason other than her daring to ask an innocent question that challenged his sense of authority. Later, he'd lash himself with his own shame and remorse.

"Well? Is that a good thing or a bad thing?" Maya finally demanded.

"I don't know. I mean, yes, he was my dad and all, but…"

"But what?"

"You know."

"I know that you need to figure out what you feel and deal with whatever is bugging you," she said bluntly. "Your dad was a good man. He loved you and your brothers. He loved me, and he loved our girls. He even loved your mom, when push came to shove. So, you need to…"

Suddenly, panic flashed through his brain like lightning in the night sky. Miles shot straight up.

"Careful!" She jerked her head back and barely dodged a bruised chin.

"Sorry! Are you alright?" He didn't wait for her to respond. "Did Parker call you today? I never called him or Benjamin."

"Wouldn't your mother have called them?"

"Who knows? She could have been too wrapped up in the inconvenience this is causing her," Miles barked, still seething with resentment at the burden Catherine placed on him.

"Oh, come on, Miles, your mom isn't a monster."

"Maybe not – but she's a pain in the ass."

He walked to the kitchen, picked up the receiver and dialed Parker, his younger brother by only sixteen months. Growing up, people often assumed they were twins. No surprise, since Catherine often dressed them alike until adolescence. Then Parker filled out so much more and so much faster than Miles that, in their teen years some people thought Parker was the older brother.

"Nope, I'm older, smarter and better looking." Miles would joke to clarify the sibling hierarchy, his tongue only partly in cheek.

Parker answered. "Hello?"

"Hey."

"Um, er…" Miles stuttered, "Did Mom call you about…"

"Dad dying? Yeah."

"Good! Wait! I don't mean 'good' that he's dead, I mean…"

"I know what you mean. She called just after you left the hospital," Parker said, his voice ragged probably from crying all day, Miles figured. Parker was a big man, and a bigger baby. Especially when it came to Michael. Miles sometimes chafed privately against Parker's worship of their father. Either Parker didn't see Michael's shortcomings or purposely ignored them. Who knew which is worse? As far as Miles cared, both are bad. However, this was no time to question or criticize his brother.

"I need to talk to you," Miles said.

"Then talk."

Growing up, it seemed Catherine tried to make them the same person (which is to say, Miles). Indeed, they'd shared a lot as boys: friends, cars, school activities. Parker even claimed he'd shared a couple of Miles' girlfriends. (Miles doubted it but could never be sure.) Yet, they were as different as Monday morning from Saturday night. Miles, the more studious, cautious and practical. Parker, more street-smart than book-smart, never shied away from a challenge or an opportunity, no matter how dangerous, reckless, unethical, or sometimes, illegal. Miles openly envied (and privately resented) his brother's adventurous spirit but had no interest in trading stability for Parker's intoxicating audacity.

"Not on the phone," Miles whispered. He peeked back at Maya on the couch, absorbed in her cross stitching.

"You don't want Maya to hear you? What's up? You got a girlfriend on the side?" He laughed.

"No, asshole. Cheating's your specialty, not mine," Miles hissed.

"Chill out! I just hoping you might introduce me." Miles could never tell when Parker was joking about such things, and his brain, raw from the day's tensions couldn't piece together the puzzle of his brother's moral code.

"C'mon, I am being serious. I just can't talk about this around her. She doesn't understand things the way you and I do," Miles explained plainly.

Like many siblings, their adolescence resonated with many shared secrets that would draw heavy reckoning from their parents (if they ever knew.) Miles and Parker built their bond as much in the dark of their shared bedroom as in the light of day. As men, they'd taken different turns down Life's path. The consequences of their choices created disagreements heavy with a dark truth that would have seemed impossible in childhood but arose in adulthood as regularly as the sun.

Still, in time of need, Miles and Parker remained close. Even gears that mesh perfectly sometimes grind. But the pool of life experience they shared could always lubricate their occasional friction.

"Ok," Parker said. "Tomorrow morning. You know where."

"Thanks."

Miles hung up. No need for further information or explanation. Brothers to the end.

8

Jordan, Illinois was the epitome of "between."

Far from both coasts and close enough to Chicago to earn the new-fangled moniker of "suburb," it was truly Middle America in the 1920s and 1930s. A key stop for travelers heading one way or another along Route 66, the mythological "Mother Road," Jordan enjoyed for many years the fuel that came with those travelers' faith in a better tomorrow.

Three generations later, the Mother Road stopped delivering dreams. Interstate highways, running long and straight and true, replaced the bifurcated blacktop of Route 66, which wandered around and through its many host towns. Where Route 66 once promised the magical charm of discovery in every small hamlet it touched, the Interstates promised one major improvement – speed.

Death loves speed. And Death – as if traveling one of those highways itself – came very quickly to Jordan.

Still, Miles loved the place. Nostalgia welled in his throat as he and Parker drove into Jordan for the first time in several months.

"Let's stop at that old greasy spoon that Dad used to take us to," Miles said.

"Are you kidding me? I'm trying to eat healthy."

Miles snorted and stared at Parker; the hypocrisy of his words as obvious as the navy-blue sweatpants struggling mightily to contain his expanding gut. Parker weighed 250 pounds if he weighed one.

"Uh-huh," Miles said, eying his brother's girth.

"I've lost fifteen pounds!" Parker patted his belly. A crooked grin parted his round face and unveiled crow's feet framing his brown eyes, a sure sign of the middle age that loomed for both.

"Really? What's her name?"

"What are you talking about?" Parker feigned surprise and indignation.

"C'mon, the only time you lose weight is when you have a new girlfriend or want one."

This had been Parker's modus operandi all the way back to their teen years. He'd slim down, seduce some new female victim – usually younger, always large breasted and often (but not always) blonde – then put on fat like a grizzly bear preparing for hibernation. Whenever the spark inevitably died, Parker would shed the weight and, soon enough, the woman.

Though sixteen months younger, Parker often looked older than Miles, partly because of the effects of a lifetime of smoking, drinking and overeating; and partly because of his prematurely snowy and thinning crown.

The combination of round belly and face and white hair (which recently spread to his whiskers) made Parker the spitting image of Santa Claus, Miles thought.

Yet the proverbial bees never stopped swarming to Parker's honey. Miles had long wondered what drew them. Parker's reputation as a "bad boy"? His gold nugget-wearing, cash-flashing lifestyle? His scent? Maybe that theory about pheromones held some water. Who knew? Miles never understood it any more than he could deny his lifelong envy.

"Man, I cannot believe you. I am really, truly losing weight because I want to be healthy. And now with Dad dying…"

"Riiiiggghht…" Miles' brow furrowed with mock sincerity.

They drove in silence for several minutes toward the east side neighborhood of their youth. The car hummed across one of the six steel bridges spanning the river that bisected Jordan and literally and symbolically separated Jordan's two communities: the older, poorer East Side and the newer, wealthier West Side.

Parker pointed at the limestone library as they passed. "Man, that place has to be at least one hundred years old. Remember when we'd ride our bikes down here?"

"No, but I remember when *I* would ride *my* bike down here. You never came closer to the library than meeting some girl outside on the lawn."

Parker smiled. "I can't help it if you were a nerd." Miles didn't respond to his attempted humor. "What's wrong?"

"Nothing, really. Just thinking about how much this place has changed."

"How do you mean?"

The car stopped at a red light at an intersection bordered by boarded store fronts, a gas station on one corner and a bar on the opposite.

"This place used to be crazy with traffic and people going downtown to shop at all the stores. Now look at it."

As recently as the 1970s, Jordan reflected the vibrant sparkle of Middle-Class Americans working hard to polish visions of a hundred new tomorrows. Now, in the late 1990s it revealed the scaly rust of a thousand yesterdays. Once again, Jordan found itself caught "between." This time, a shifting economy, burst financial bubbles and the corporate greed of the 1980s pinched the town.

Miles surveyed the sidewalks, more populated with litter than people. Three vagrants loitered near the bus stop. A fourth slept beneath a newspaper on the bench inside the passenger shelter. The plastic shell, once clear, stood opaque with the scars of generations of graffiti.

"No one comes here anymore, unless it's to go home after work." Miles stared out the window at a freight train ambling slowly along its elevated track above the street half a block away. Most of the cars boasted more spray-painted scrawling than contents.

"Remember how there used to be so many trains at night? They'd go by so often we couldn't sleep without the noise when we spent weekends at Grandma and Grandpa's house."

They laughed.

"And all those trains bringing steel to the mills, oil, cars, food…" Miles' voice trailed off as he stared vacantly ahead. "Now, the only thing they bring is traffic delays."

"Wow, you really are in a shitty mood." Parker said. "If you didn't want to come down here, we could have gone somewhere else. You're the one who wanted to meet up. I would have been happy to talk on the phone."

The light turned green. Miles edged through the intersection and past a three-quarters empty shopping center. Cracks in the crumbling asphalt parking lot showed through melting snow in the areas where abandoned cars weren't parked or tractor trailers didn't rest under light stanchions, their bulbs shot out long ago. A prototype of what became known as a "department store" anchored the strip mall when the Ayalas dominated the neighborhood in the 1960s and 1970s. The shopping center provided adventure when they'd walk to the stores with Michael as children, and later, as adolescents when they earned the privilege to walk there alone.

Now, a ghost of its former suburban glory, a few tenants still scraped and scuffled, clinging to life against odds inconceivable only thirty short years ago.

"No, not really," Miles said. "I really do love this place. This is still home to me. I mean, look at those stores. If they were humans, they'd have black eyes and bloody noses, but they're still standing. There's a 'survivor spirit' here that those rich SOB's on the West Side can't understand. I'm proud of growing up here.

Proud of being an Ayala. But…"

"But what?

"I'm…I don't know…Just mad about how things have turned out."

Uncertainty clouded Parker's face. "What are you talking about? You're mad because of the way the old neighborhood looks?"

"No, not that …"

"Well, what then? Jesus, I'm really confused."

"Me, too. About you, and me, and Dad. And I figured the best place to try to sort it out is where everything started."

Miles pulled into the parking lot behind the shopping center and turned the car toward the row of dilapidated houses facing the loading docks. Miles stared at the old house that moored their childhood from the days when Miles could barely walk and Parker still wore diapers, until the nights when the topic of girls consumed almost all their nighttime conversation in the bedroom they shared. The house once felt like the biggest thing on the entire block, overflowing with energy and activity and sound and light. Now it had somehow shrunk and grown quiet, tired somehow, and dark. Even in the bright sunlight of a January Saturday morning. Miles shifted into "park" and turned to his brother, his lifelong confidante and (though he often hated to admit it) his spiritual, if sometimes evil twin.

Parker turned in the passenger seat to look at Miles. "Seriously man, you have got to stop talking in circles. You're making my head hurt. What is wrong?"

"Did you know Mom asked me to do the eulogy?"

"No."

"Does that bother you?"

"Why should it? You're the oldest son. You're the big shot writer and professional talker. You know if Mom or Benjamin gets up there it'll just be a disaster. And you know I'll probably be getting busy with one of our cousins!"

Miles ignored Parker's typically-poorly-timed joke.

"That's just it. I don't know if I am his son. Or if I even want to be."

His eyes dropped to the seat. The same tension as he'd felt at the hospital enveloped him again. Once more, Miles felt trapped.

Between duty and irritation.

Past and present.

Certainty and confusion.

Love and anger.

Between.

<u>9</u>

Miles knew Parker's every look.

A lifetime of mutual familiarity made Parker's face an emotional billboard. Each wrinkle, smile, squint, frown, stare, eye roll and twitch broadcast Parker's heart to his brother so precisely that they often didn't have to use actual words to express their feelings.

For example, Miles knew that, true to his ample girth, Parker did most things in large ways. He wore flashy jewelry. When he had any, he spent money lavishly on his current companion, family and friends. And he could often be heard above the din of a party crowd, booming obscenity-laced jokes, bragging about (and scavenging financial support for) his latest business, or practicing his sexual voodoo on yet another unwitting female victim. In the latter two situations, Miles would often think, "Run, sucker!"

But in anger, Parker was a man of small gestures.

An arched right eyebrow tipped his displeasure - an affectation he stole from their father. He rarely raised his voice. His soft tone and even cadence disguised his irritation. Michael used the same psychological gimmick as a cop to get suspects to feel comfortable. Drop their guard. Trust him. Confess. Parker used it in his shady business dealings for much the same reason. *One a cop, the other a con man…and you never knew if either of them ever told the truth…*

Now, Parker sat two feet away compressed in the passenger seat, propped against the door and turned toward the middle of the car. He tried to push his seat back but couldn't bend down far enough to catch the release bar. His head dipped, then rose. His mocha eyes stared through the knife-edged slits of his puffy eyelids, his lips drew tightly back, canine-like, over clenched teeth. *Here it comes…*

Parker's eyebrow peaked. His volume dropped

"What the fuck is wrong with you?" Soft, low, smooth, almost serene.

Miles, for whom melodrama was a constant and regular companion, fired back at full volume. "What's wrong with *me*? Are you kidding? And watch your language, for Christ's sake."

"Fuck" …pause… "You. Is my language OK for you now, Princess? You say you don't know if you're Dad's son and you expect me to just sit here and listen to that crap? I'm asking you again: what the fuck is wrong with you?"

"Look, I don't know what I am feeling right now, and…"

"Bullshit. You keep repeating that, but you dragged me all the way down here. Stop being such a pussy. Just say whatever it is and stop wasting my time." Parker twisted again in his seat, unable to align his bulk with Miles.

"Fine. I don't want to do the goddamn eulogy because I cannot stand up there in front of who knows how many people who all think Dad walked on water and tell the truth."

"The truth? Like how he adopted us and gave us his name when mom was raising us practically alone? Everyone knows and no one gives a shit. We're his sons the same as Benji, and probably more in some ways."

"No, I mean the truth. Like how he wasn't a good person. At least not as good as everyone thinks and wants to believe."

Parker tried to lift his left leg but winced in pain when his knee wouldn't bend. Calmly, he said, "What the hell are you talking about? First, no one is perfect. Second, you don't have to tell his whole life story. Just get up there and say a few things about what a great cop he was and a terrific dad and a wonderful husband. I don't get what is so hard."

Miles exploded. "That's what I'm saying! He may have been a great cop and a decent father, but not a wonderful husband. He was terrible to Mom and I am not - I CANNOT - stand up there and lie with her sitting ten feet away, knowing what I know."

"'Knowing what you know'? What does that mean? What are you, the CIA now? What do you think you know?"

Miles nearly spit his exasperation. "How can you say that with a straight face? He physically and emotionally abused Mom."

Parker scoffed.

"Oh, come on!" Miles yelled. "I have never met a bigger racist, especially considering he is, I mean, *was* Mexican himself. Remember when we were in high school and Shaun Williams came over for dinner? Dad kept making jokes about counting the silverware and talking like one of the field hands in *Gone with the Wind*?" Miles effected a Southern drawl. "'Yassa Mr. Williams! I sho' will be servin' you up some mo' chicken!' Ya'll want some wata-melon wit' dat'? Real goddamn funny! I was so embarrassed for our friend and ashamed of Dad."

"Ok," Parker consented, "but that's how guys, and cops were back then. 'Old school.' They all acted like that. C'mon…remember Big Bobby calling Dad a taco bender and Frito Bandito, and all the detectives pretending to be in the Mafia whenever Deputy DiBenedetto was around? Those were different times."

Miles' face twisted with disgust. "Are you kidding me? Jesus Christ! The racism is the least of it. He was nasty and mean and critical to anyone he didn't like and for no good reason. Jesus Himself could have come to our door and Dad would have slammed the door in His face because he didn't like His long hair or sandals."

"So what?" Parker said. "He didn't like long-haired hippie freaks."

"C'mon Parker, you know what I mean. If he didn't like you, he would never like you no matter what. But if he did, then you could do anything, and it wouldn't matter. Remember when that disgusting, filthy informant came to our door during dinner?"

Parker smiled. "I remember."

"The guy looked like Charles Manson escaped. For all we knew, he could have been an ax murderer and now he knew where we lived. But Dad liked him, so it didn't matter what anyone else thought," Miles said. "And it really, I mean *really* pisses me off that you're sitting here defending him when he was no better to you. Christ, he almost killed you once!"

"Jesus, are you out your mind? When did he almost kill me?" Parker said, his tone thickening now with incredulity.

"Are you serious? Now you're going to pretend that you don't remember how bad he beat you when you drove his squad car around the block when you were thirteen? You had so many welts on your ass you looked like Kunta Kinte from 'Roots'! If Mom hadn't pulled him off you, you might be dead now."

"Yeah, but…" Parker started.

"Yeah, but what? You deserved it? I agree! What a stupid thing to do, on about a million levels. You could have killed yourself or someone else, not to mention getting Dad in a lot of trouble.

Parker couldn't hide the smile that creased his face as he turned and looked out the door window. "Yeah, that was kind of fun though, especially when I turned on the red lights and called to that homeless guy over the loudspeaker. 'Hey! You're under arrest for being a bum!'"

"The way I remember it, Dad sure as hell didn't find it amusing."

"See, this is your problem," Parker countered. "Your whole life, you overreact to everything. No one got hurt and Dad didn't get in any trouble."

"No, but only because of dumb luck! To make matters worse, you ran away, and Mom had to call the police - Dad's friends - to find you. And then lie !" Exasperation fueled new anger over the decades-old incident.

"Well he made me mad! I just wanted to be a cop like him," Parker explained.

"I don't know. Maybe Mom shouldn't have stopped him from beating you. Apparently, it did no good. You're just as big an asshole as Dad." Miles no longer even tried to contain his fury. "I am embarrassed to be associated with him, much less related to him. If I could choose a man to be my father, it sure as hell wouldn't be a man like him."

"Alright, alright." Parker's words struck an unintended tone of condescension.

"Don't fucking talk down to me, like I am making all this shit up! I can't understand why you don't understand," Miles demanded. Then, sarcastically feigning sudden clarity, as if the answer had burst from the air around them: "Oh, but of course! Now I get it. Michael Ayala is your hero! Your perfect role model! He couldn't possibly do anything wrong in your fucking eyes, could he? It didn't matter how many people he hurt."

Miles turned away from Parker and stared out the car window. He glimpsed his face in the door mirror. Red-partitioned eyes, heavy and dull with the weight of a sleepless night; unshaven, gaunt cheeks; disheveled hair, seemingly more salt than pepper. *Jesus, I look like shit!* Like a movie poltergeist, an ache crept from his shoulders, up the back of his neck and took permanent residency at the top of his skull. Blood throbbed in his ears and his chest felt like he'd been punched.

Parker tried to wipe away the condensation glazing the inside of the windshield, but his paunch spilled into the space between him and the dash, so that he couldn't reach the glass.

Losing weight, my ass…

A shroud of rage enveloped Miles. Each invisible cord tightened around his neck, over his head, choking off his breath.

Suddenly an ear-splitting noise filled the car. Miles was surprised to realize it was his own voice. It started as a low-pitched growl, then rose, one letter at a time, to a piercing scream, giving the single-syllable word more weight than usual. "Ffffuuuuucccccckkkk!" He grabbed the steering wheel and shook crazily, back and forth, strangling the life out of the lifeless leather-covered victim.

"Jesus Christ!" Parker yelled, eyes bulging with astonishment at the outburst. He reached across the seat, but Miles sharply slapped Parker's hand away.

He glared at his younger brother, his mirror image, his lifelong shoulder and ear, his shared soul. *Finally, you show some goddamn emotion!* The words took shape in his head, but Miles could not force them to his lips. Confusion paralyzed him; fear for what he might do next kept him glued to his seat.

"Calm down! Come on, chill out!" Parker ordered. "I know you're upset, but this isn't doing any good. You're just steaming up the windows." He tried yet again to maneuver around and find a comfortable position in the constricting passenger seat. "Let's get out of this car before I lose all circulation in my balls. Can't you get a bigger car?"

"Can't you get a smaller ass!?" Miles shot back.

A pause…a space in time…a second of silence…pure and clear and perfect. Much later, Miles would recall and reflect on this moment to try to understand what happened next. As with other times when obvious rationality failed, he defaulted to the irrational. Simple, unquestioning faith in the mysterious often provides the best explanation for life's mysteries. "Sometimes God speaks loudest in the silence," he would think. Maybe this was one of those times.

Whatever the reason, a few seconds later, Miles grinned. A single snicker led to several chuckles. Parker followed and soon, peals of laughter pushed the silence aside. The storm of rage evaporated as suddenly as it appeared. The brothers laughed until the laughter expelled all the air from their lungs. They desperately gasped for air, struggling to regain control of their bodies now aching from their irrational hysterics. They lost that battle, happily, for several minutes.

Finally, when their breath returned and they could look at each other without spontaneously cracking up, each opened their car door. The January morning air bit their bare cheeks, but provided a good tonic for the stale, steamy carbon dioxide-filled atmosphere in the car.

"C'mon." Parker threw his fat, stubby arm around his big brother. "Let's take a walk."

10

A wooden spoon banged against a metal pot and a blender whirred to life, backed by a twangy Kenny Chesney song. The smell of onions and garlic danced across the living room and drew Miles through the front door.

Food well-made could be as sensual and seductive as sex – and sometimes more rewarding and memorable. Miles liked to eat. Maya liked to cook. *It's a marriage made in culinary heaven,* he often joked.

He hung up his coat, removed his shoes and crept toward the kitchen. Miles leaned on the door post but did not announce his presence. Maya stood at the counter, back to the door. Wearing loose-fitting pajamas, her backside swaying lightly to the music, she was deep into what Miles called a "Major Cook" – making several dishes to be frozen for nights when making dinner would be too much work. Though certainly not averse to the occasional burger in a bag, Maya preferred homemade and healthy to eating out. So, every few weeks she'd spend half the day in the kitchen. Miles silently stared at her, taking all of her in, and smiled.

How did I get so lucky? he thought, for the millionth time. Then, "Hey, that smells great! What are you making?"

Maya turned, grinning. She did not seem startled at all. Had she known he was there, staring at her, the whole time? He wouldn't put it past her. Maya was proud of her femininity- well aware of the effect it had on her husband and unashamed to use it.

"Oh, hi hon," she said in a casual, sing-song voice. "Just a few things for down the road. I made that cream of chicken soup you like so much, the one with the wild rice. And I'm making chili now."

His eyes widened with anticipation and appreciation. "Have I told you lately that I love you?"

He took two steps, turned her toward him, ran his hands over her full hips, and kissed her, slowly. She must have just sampled her work. *Chili spices… Mmmm…*

Maya broke the embrace after a few seconds. "Wow! All that for soup and chili?"

She was a good inch shorter than Miles. Her short hair now hinted at the white that had commandeered her mother's head as a very young woman. Maya didn't mindlessly follow every fashion trend like bloodhounds after an elusive scent - bleached hair, breast implants, Botox, tanning salons - only to see their looks crumble under the hammer of time. Age softened her in a way that bolstered her natural good looks. Like one of those paintings that, when you stand close, you see is made up of thousands of little pictures, Maya was a complex work of art. A rare and mysterious mixture of intelligence, wit and personal contentment. A mature, selfless soul and, most important, a profoundly nurturing spirit. Other women may be more physically striking. But none were as essentially beautiful as his wife, Miles thought.

"Not just that. You know better."

He wrapped his arms around her again and buried his head in her neck, nibbling that spot that made her giggle, just in the crease above her shoulder. He knew how to get a woman going – especially this one – and liked to remind her every now and again that he was a healthy male. She returned the hug, then gently pushed away.

Turning her back to him as she returned to the stove Maya stirred a pan of ground beef. "So how did it go with your brother? Do you feel better now about things?"

"Well, those are two separate questions." He stole a handful of the diced, raw green pepper at Maya's right side. "These are sweet!"

Maya slapped his hand. "Ok, answer the first one."

"It was fine. Parker makes me so mad sometimes, but he always makes me laugh. We walked around the neighborhood and talked about a lot of things. Mostly about growing up there."

"What about it?"

"You know. Everything. We walked down to Grandma's house. It sure looks a lot smaller now than when we were kids."

"Everything always does."

For most of their childhood, Michael and Catherine had rented a house surrounded by other Ayalas. So many extended family members lived within walking distance that friends – before Political Correctness reared its ugly head – called the area "Taco Hill."

Miles crossed the kitchen. He leaned backwards against the table's edge, arms folded.

"I know what you mean, but it's strange seeing something one way as a child and seeing it completely differently now. It's, I don't know, it's kind of disconcerting. Like when you put on someone else's glasses who's got a stronger prescription. Your brain knows you're looking at the same things - that's my table, that's my chair - but your eyes can't quite focus, or the depth perception is off. I don't know…something. It's just wrong. And a little sad."

"That just means you're getting older," Maya teased.

Miles was six months her senior to the day, but she loved treating him as if he had one foot in the grave. Especially when this air of melodramatic nostalgia took over. Humor usually brought him back to reality without hurting his feelings.

Miles laughed at her good-natured jab.

He'd shared this story often. So often, Maya once finished it for him which, he secretly thought, was a bit irritating. He remembered thinking at the time, "Don't steal my spotlight like that." Still he knew his wife bore an unlimited supply of patience. He knew she understood he needed tell it one more time, hoping the repetition would lighten the weight pressing so heavily on his spirit. He knew her kind heart and loved her for it.

"Yea, but in my mind, I guess, that neighborhood will always be what it was when we were kids."

Theirs had been a poor block in the poor part of town, but a definite air of pride balanced the poverty.

"The houses might have showed their age, you know what I mean? One might have been missing a shingle or two, or had a torn screen, but everyone did their best to keep everything looking good, at least," Miles explained. "The yards were small, and there may have been a few weeds here and there, but the lawns were always mowed. We had gardens with flowers and vegetables in the back. Nothing fancy, just something to brighten everything up and give us a few things to eat so that you didn't have to always run to the store. Beans and corn and tomatoes, maybe some cucumbers. That's when I learned to love gardening. To this day, nothing tastes as good as a tomato picked from the garden that you helped grow!" A proud smile creased his face.

"And I'll tell you something else," he continued. "There may have been a lot of toys and bikes scattered around. No one much cared about that. Kids are kids, and I think the adults liked all the noise and mess that they made. I think it somehow reminded them of the joy that had been sucked out of their lives."

"Miles! It wasn't that bad."

"Maybe not for you where you grew up, but on my side of town, there could be a lot of sadness. Still, no matter what else was going on, everyone took care of their little corner of the world. There was no litter in the gutters, like you see now. No spare tires leaning against the houses for everyone to see. And you better not let any gravel get on the sidewalk! It stayed in the driveway if you knew what was good for you!" Rueful laughter filled the kitchen. Appearances, Miles knew, mean a lot to people who have little else.

"But the best part was Grandma and Grandpa Ayala's house. It was right on our way to school, so we'd stop over there every day. Grandpa was always working in his garden out back, in and out of that tarpaper shed for this thing or that. He was retired by the time we came along, so he was always working those vegetables, bent over, picking tomatoes or pulling weeds. I was in, it had to be, maybe third grade? Parker was in first. You could walk to and from school back then without anyone messing with you. Of course, it helped that our dad was a cop and the whole area was family..."

He winked a giant stage wink, silently hinting at the "Old Days" when cops protected their own without question or consequence.

"We would come home from school and stop at Grandma Ayala's house. She was already very old by the time Mom and Dad got married. Maybe in her eighties. She probably knew about twenty words of English, but we could always understand her well enough. She'd be sitting in her chair when we came in. Her glasses magnified her eyes. She always wore a scarf on her head – a babushka, my mom called it – and an apron. I never saw her without an apron. When I kissed her cheek, she'd grab my face with both hands and she'd say, 'I lav ju my little Miles', in her broken English. She always smelled like, I don't know... bread dough and talcum powder...kind of sweet and earthy at the same time."

Miles paused again as memories long packed away unfolded themselves.

"Then she'd grab her walker, get up, go into the kitchen" - Miles demonstrated his paternal grandmother's step-stop, step-stop, step-stop gait - "and make us homemade tortillas. Nothing ever came out of a bag there! She'd pat and flip them all in one motion, add a touch of flour, then put them directly on the burner and turn them with her bare fingers. Just until they started to show little brown spots. That's how you knew they were done. And man, did they taste delicious! One time my poor grandpa asked, 'Why you no make for me?' Grandma yelled at him in Spanish and shoo-ed him away. He mumbled something we couldn't understand, threw his hands in the air and went back outside. I don't know what she said, but you could tell exactly what she meant. Those tortillas were special, for us. My aunt always said Grandma loved us just like any of her other grandchildren…but I think maybe she loved us a little more. Because we were my Dad's sons. And everyone knew that he was her favorite because he was the baby."

"Then she'd put butter on the tortillas, fold them up for us, kiss us and send us on our way. Parker always ran out of there with two or three extras in his fat hands like he stole something – surprise, surprise." Miles' rolling eyes emphasized his sarcasm. "We had so much fun there."

He stared at the kitchen table without clarifying if he'd meant that morning, or twenty-five years before. Excited now by the familiar tale's re-telling, the fire of happy memories sparkled in his eyes. Homemade tortillas were only the smallest sliver of a lifetime of wonderful smells and tastes and sounds that he'd never had known if not for this new "Familia" that he inherited through Michael Ayala.

Maya interrupted his reverie, trying to steer the conversation off Memory Lane and back to the main road. "So, what did you and Parker fight about?"

"The usual."

Maya gently pressed him to clarify. "Honey, with you and Parker, 'The Usual' could be a million things. Can you be more specific?"

Miles exhaled, seemingly exhausted from having to explain yet again a concept that seemed simple enough to him. He spoke slowly, as if to a baby. "He thinks Dad walked on water and that I should do the eulogy and just be done with it."

Maya did not raise her eyes from the soup simmering on the burner.

Miles suddenly knew he'd crossed a line and he should back off. Maya usually indulged his whip-snapping emotions, tolerant to a fault. Yet she'd made it abundantly clear in past arguments that she didn't appreciate her husband's condescension which tended to appear when he got mad or felt stressed, threatened or challenged.

"Hey, don't talk to me like that. I am not an idiot. I just asked a question," she said.

"Honey, I know, but I've been telling you this for two days now. I don't know why it's so hard to understand. I don't want to do Dad's eulogy." He sat down at the table, hoping to offer a quick apology and easy explanation.

"But why?"

"Because…"

"Because why?"

"Because I don't feel much like his son. I don't have his blood, we didn't share any interests, we were different kinds of people. I don't like the way he treated my mom and I don't want to be the kind of man he was. Is that clear enough for you?"

He stared at Maya, waiting for a response. An acknowledgement. Validation of his feelings.

None came.

"You know…" The words issued quietly, calmly from the woman with whom he'd shared every waking moment for more than a decade; the person to whom he'd promised eternal love, the mother of his children, but he knew that their peace was illusory. "For a person as smart as you are, sometimes you are an idiot."

"Wait a minute…"

"A jerk!" Maya shook the spoon at him, flinging ground beef in his direction. "A complete asshole!"

"Now that's not fair!"

"Not fair?" Her eyes normally set at an alluring half-mast, now opened wide with fury. "I will tell you what's not fair. That I've been walking on eggshells for two days now because you're pissed off. I have put up with your whining because of all this B.S. about your dad being a bad guy, you not feeling close to him, blah, blah, blah…"

She paused. Miles remained silent. He knew it was best to just wait out the storm. Her second round detonated like a hand grenade at close range.

"Here's a newsflash for you: No one is perfect!"
Maya exploded, her reprimand overpowering poor
Kenny Chesney's soft Tennessee warble. "Not your dad,
not me, and especially not *you*. What it really comes
down to is, this is interfering with your precious 'world
order.' God forbid that anything isn't exactly perfect as
defined by the Great and Powerful Miles Ayala. You
might have to do something out of the ordinary, and that
would inconvenience you."

She took another step toward him. Miles didn't dare
move.

"Honey, I love you, but sometimes you can be so
incredibly arrogant. You think everything is about you,
and what isn't about you, should be about you. Well, I
am sorry to say, that's not the way the real world works."
Each angry word became a stiletto, their truth drawing
blood until he had to turn away to avoid her sharp stare.
"Unfortunately, your dad died way too young. He wasn't
the best father or the greatest husband ever, and you're
hurt about that. I get it. But," Maya inched closer with
each breath, "It's NOT ABOUT YOU!"

Miles reached out and tried to put his hand on her
hip. The spoon whistled sharply and cracked against his
fingers. "Ouch!" he yelped.

"Oh, did that hurt my baby? Good!" Maya scolded,
not even a hint of forgiveness in her voice. "You know
who else is hurting right now? Your mom. I know I am
not particularly close to her. But I also know how I
would feel if you went to work one morning and
suddenly died. I'd feel lost and afraid and confused and
angry at everyone. And believe it or not, I might even

feel like I could use some help and support from my children. I promise, you won't die from doing a eulogy."

His head dipped, heavy with guilt. She was right. He could be what some charitably called "difficult." Short on patience and long on temper, Miles demanded perfection from everyone around him, as well as himself. He easily chafed when his version of perfection (which, in his mind, was the only version) didn't materialize, and did little to disguise his cynicism and disappointment. Most of all, he didn't like to be challenged and hated repeating himself to anyone. Once, he made the arrogant mistake of letting his ego wander too far without a leash, telling Maya, "I'm bright, talented, creative, witty and confident. I just don't understand why others don't understand that I know best and just do what I say." She punched him, hard, in the chest. The fist-shaped bruise didn't fade for a week.

Still, he'd learned early in their courting he could not win against Maya. Mostly because she was almost always right - a fact he tried to humorously deflect rather than openly admit. He pulled out his white handkerchief and waved it in front of his face. "Ok, Ok, I surrender!"

Maya sighed and stepped back, failing to muffle a chuckle at the gesture.

"It's just that I don't like change," he continued. "Change means chaos, and chaos means I'm not in control. And this whole situation just screams 'out of control!' I can't stand funerals. The idea of having to greet all those people, listening to their platitudes about my dad – 'Oh, Michael is so great!' - and the reception after. I mean, really: is there anything more awkward than a funeral reception? Not to mention having to go through all of Dad's stuff later…what a pain in the ass."

His head ached again with the thought.

"That's all well and good, and I appreciate you being honest with me, and yourself." Her softer tone implied forgiveness, but it was short-lived. "Still, you really need to work on your control issues, Mister. I don't know what this is about, but I know in my heart that it's a whole lot more than what you're saying. Maybe you don't even know yourself. But right now, you need to go call your mother and tell her that you are ready to help. That's what she needs right now, and you need to think about someone other than yourself."

Miles sighed. Fatigued from fighting, embarrassed, mad at himself for his emotional shortcomings, he lifted himself from the kitchen chair. Shoulders drooping, feet dragging, he trudged to the living room, picked up the phone and dialed Catherine's number.

The rings sounded somehow far away. Finally, she picked up.

"Hey Mom, it's me…"

11

The front door to his parents' house swung open easily.

Jesus, why don't they ever lock this door? Miles thought for what he was sure was the millionth time. He never understood why a police officer wouldn't do everything he could to secure his house and family, knowing what the world outside held. Or was it just the opposite? That he felt no need to take extra precaution because people somehow knew what waited inside for anyone who dared violate Michael Ayala's trust. Take his possessions. Hurt his family. Seen that way, locks seemed superfluous. Either way, Miles was in a gray mood as he stepped into his parents' – or, now, he corrected himself, his mother's – home.

An ornate, antique wooden shadow box hung on the wall near the front door. Each Christmas for as long as he could remember, Catherine had painstakingly created a magnificent winter village of blown glass buildings, churches and foliage. Miniature, hand-painted glass revelers rode in tiny horse-drawn sleighs or skied down hills of snowy cotton flowing from the top of a display shelf to the gold-painted bottom of the shadow box. Twinkling lights lining the box bounced their sparkle from the mirror behind, giving the whole scene a mid-winter's eve glow. As he had done countless times growing up, he admired that shadow box, amazed by and proud of Catherine's creativity, and her dedication to this little fantasy world.

He closed the front door, secured the lock, and called in. "Ma, I'm here." No answer. He stomped the snow off his shoes on the carpet just inside the door, took one step to the left, peered up the stairs and listened. No noise. "Ma? Where are you?" *Did she go out somewhere knowing I was coming?* The drive between his home in Westville and Jordan was only about forty minutes, depending on traffic. Not that far. Yet still long enough to be inconvenient, especially if Thought was the only distraction from the driving, as it was today. And Thought, normally Miles' best friend, resource and stock in trade had become his irritating personal Public Enemy Number One in the three days since Michael had died. Too many thoughts swimming randomly through his brain, trailing phosphorescent emotional flotsam in their wake.

He removed his shoes and walked heavily down the short hall to the dining room. The walls were a photographic museum of his parents, himself and his brothers ending at the dining room door leading to the basement. He called from the top of the stairs. "Ma! Are you down there?"

Catherine's head appeared from around the corner,

floating at the bottom like a detached spirit. "I didn't hear you come in. I'll be up in a minute." As usual her greeting failed to acknowledge the possibility that a rapist, thief or murderer could have been standing in her kitchen instead of her oldest child.

Miles turned and sat at the kitchen table. He sifted through a handful of sympathy cards scattered around a vase of condolence flowers. The usual store-bought sentiments – "Praying for you in your time of grieving…So sorry for your loss…Heartfelt wishes for comfort…May your heart find peace during this difficult time…" Fewer than he'd have expected, given the immense number of Michael's family, friends and associates. Then Miles remembered that it was only Monday. Michael'd died on Friday, no mail on Sunday. These were just the first wave, from the most immediate friends and family. He tossed the cards back as Catherine reached the top of the stairs with a full laundry basket in hand. He rose. "Want me to take that upstairs for you?"

"No, I have to iron some things first. I'll do it after you leave." Catherine emitted her family-infamous "The weight of the world is on my shoulders" sigh. She set the basket at the foot of the ironing board – he could not remember a time growing up when it was not standing and at the ready – in the family room adjacent to the kitchen and circled back to the refrigerator. "Sit down," she ordered. "Do you want something to eat or drink?"

Always the martyr…

"No, I'm fine," Miles said. "I mean, I am not fine, but I'm not hungry."

"Well then, what's wrong?" She stepped toward the

table. Her gaze bounced around the kitchen to the laundry basket in the next room, then back to Miles.

He stood from his chair, the table between them. He turned, stepped a few feet away, then returned to the table as if tethered to the spot. He grabbed the back of the chair, eyes locked on the condolence cards. "I don't know how to say this…" Of course, he did know how to say it. He just didn't want to, fully expecting the "Universe as He Knew It" to now explode at his words.

Another slightly annoyed sigh. "Miles, what is it? I have a lot to do."

As he learned to do twenty years ago playing the clarinet and saxophone, Miles dropped his diaphragm, expanding his belly to fill his lungs. He pinched closed his nostrils and lips. Held his breath for what felt like minutes, hours, days…then exhaled, gut compressing, expelling the last vestiges of air from his lungs – and taking with it any chance of retreat.

He lifted his eyes and stared squarely at Catherine, noting, not for the first time, how piercing her stare could be, then blurted: "I know you're not going to like this, but I don't want to do Dad's eulogy."

Catherine crossed the kitchen. Her house slippered footsteps produced the only sound as they softly swooshed across the hardwood floor. She sat and lowered her eyes. Her head followed into her cupped hands where it rested for what felt like a noiseless eternity. Catherine comprised an amalgam of many things both pleasant and unpleasant. At turns both fascinating and frustrating, but always predictable. Loud and boisterous when happy, she injected herself into every space, dominating conversations and commanding center stage like a performer rescuing a dying bit. When sad, though, she cried inconsolably. Anger yielded razor-edged language, self-pitying histrionics and enough melodrama to fill one hundred bad soap operas. But total silence? Miles never saw this before. He quietly stepped backward to open more space between himself and Catherine, unsure what to expect.

"Mom, I'm sorry. I know you have good reasons for wanting me to do this, but I just can't."

Finally, she dropped her hands and stared at him. Tears hidden behind her fingers had created mascara rivulets down her cheek. "Why not?" she said, her tone unusually and disarmingly soft.

Miles sat across the table from his mother, sensing a chance to talk freely through a window of calm unexpectedly but gratefully open. "It's hard to explain."

"Explain," she ordered, still calm, but firm. Even at her best, Catherine did not suffer fools with anything resembling gladness.

Miles quickly arranged and rearranged words that danced in his head for several days. Trying to order them just so, wanting to make clear his feelings yet still respect Catherine. Nothing and no one – and certainly not her eldest child – could rightfully diminish, even slightly, much less disregard her feelings, no matter how self-serving, irrational or downright wrong they may be. Facts are immutable, but Truth, (with a capital "T") shifts on the personal and relative sands of philosophy, religion, politics and circumstance, Miles knew. Reality changed shape to fit its context, like cake batter filling a form.

Catherine's feelings about Michael changed over the years. Miles saw it himself. Watched as love became appreciation became complacency became tolerance became disgust became self and shared loathing became…something between resentment and resignation. Something he couldn't name but which allowed a shared life to splinter. Fragmented to its roots, surviving in a state that no longer demands nor expects love. Miles didn't pretend to know every detail of his parents' married life, but he knew enough to understand his mother's perspective on most things – mainly because she never stopped publicizing her emotional state whether he (or anyone else) wanted to know or not. Still, he could not peg her feelings at this moment. Sadness? Grief? Loneliness? Relief? Joy? Confusion? Fear? All reasonable, he knew. All justified.

Miles drew a breath to fan the flame of his confidence, then spoke, the words tiptoe-ing out of his mouth like soldiers stepping into an unfamiliar field, certain from experience that landmines exist, but not knowing what will set them off.

"I've given this a lot of thought in the last few days. Heck, for a long time, truth be told. I loved Dad, but I can't stand in front of a room full of his family and friends and say that he was such a *'great guy.'*" His fingers formed "air quotes" around the last two words.

"Why not?" Catherine stared at her eldest son through dry eyes.

He breathed deeply. Her deep, brown eyes edged by baby crow's feet, inevitable with the approach of middle age but less than one might expect, remained fixed on his. Her lips clamped over her teeth, offering neither smile nor frown. No sign to betray whatever was going through her mind.

Sensing understanding, Miles plunged ahead. "Because I'd be lying. And I won't lie. About this or anything else."

With that bit of candor, he felt as if a thousand pounds lifted off his back. *Success! That wasn't as bad as I thought it would be…*

Catherine slowly stood, stepped away and paced between the sink and the table. Then, nearly whispering, she turned back to Miles. "Today is Monday. The funeral is Thursday. I have enough to deal with without you getting all 'High and Mighty' on me. I need your help. You are the only person I can trust to do this the right way."

"Mom, please. Parker or Benjamin can do it…"

"No!" She exploded, morphing in a flash into a thundering, lightning-spewing storm. "You are the oldest child. It's *your* job!"

"But that's my point!" Miles interrupted. "I don't feel like his child and…"

The conversation, inasmuch as Catherine ever indulged in actual dialogue with anyone, ended. She now heard only her own words, each sentence louder than the last. "I haven't asked you or your brothers to do anything since your dad died and now, I am asking for one favor – one goddamned favor that will make my life a whole lot easier. But I wouldn't want to burden *you* with anything! *Heaven forbid!*" Catherine snapped. "Not like I've been burdened all of my life. Not like I have had to do everything, taking care of everyone in my life since I was nine years old!"

Now there's the Mom I know.

Catherine grabbed a cereal bowl still half-filled with the morning's breakfast and threw it at the sink. Milk and shards of cereal-covered glass exploded across the counter and floor. "I sacrificed my entire life for you boys, giving up my own dreams, marrying a drunken loser who almost killed me and then marrying your dad so that you and Parker would have a father!"

Miles couldn't stomach any more. He shot out of the chair as if he'd been ejected from an airplane and screamed. "Oh, for Christ's sake! I am so goddamned sick and tired of hearing how you gave up everything for us! I am grateful that we had a dad…" he stretched each word to make them longer, heavier with the weight of emphasis "…but when will you ever take responsibility for your own choices? I am truly, sincerely sorry you've had a shitty life. I *know* you had a rough childhood. I know you and your stepmom didn't get along. I know kids teased you in school because you were so poor. And I know you had a horrible first marriage. But we didn't cause any of that. We didn't ask you to marry Dad! You've beat us up with this our whole lives, but I was one and Parker was an infant. It's not our fault!"

Miles knew his words were painful (though true). Still, he couldn't stop. He heard them coming from his mouth, yet they seemed disconnected. Ethereal. As if coming from someone else. "You cannot hold us hostage for the rest of our lives because you made bad choices. If anyone is to blame for anything, I blame the two of you for turning Parker and me into some kind of freak half-breeds! White kids with Mexican names, not Mexican, but treated like we were. My whole life, people looking down at us, calling us names, mocking us. Some people gave us crap because they thought we were Mexican, and others gave us crap because we weren't *really* Mexican. 'You don't *look* like an Ayala! Huh, huh, huh!'" he sneered, repeating the phrase heard so many times through childhood and adolescence. "Assholes! We didn't fit in anywhere!" Miles sucked air through his clenched teeth and wound up again.

"Do you know that one time a girl's mother told her daughter that she couldn't date me because they didn't want her dating a 'wetback'?"

"Oh Miles, she didn't really…"

"Yes, she did!" he quickly countered. "I heard her say it in the background over the phone. Christ, it's bad enough to be discriminated against for something that you are. But to be beat up for something you're not? None of those 'traditional minorities' have anything on me, boy. To make matters worse you wouldn't let us take bilingual classes so we could at least *learn* Spanish. I almost lost my first newspaper job because someone from the Westville Hispanic Chamber of Commerce got pissed off and complained to the publisher because I didn't speak the language. I mean, did it ever occur to you what you were setting us up for?" Miles demanded. "And none of this even begins to touch on how he treated you all those years. Belittling you. Making fun of you. Hitting you. And worst of all, cheating on you! Jesus, if that's not the definition of 'abusive' then I don't know what is!"

Catherine drew a sharp breath. Her eyes widened with surprise. "You know about the cheating?"

"Of course, I do! So does Parker. All those nights and weekends away, we knew they weren't all work. We were kids, but we weren't stupid. And then when he tried to bring her to his own mother's funeral? Are you kidding me? So yeah, if anyone is to blame for anything, I blame him for tricking you into marrying him and creating a bullshit world around us just so that he could have his little built-in family and look like a big shot to everyone. I don't know who I am, and I don't know who he was. But I do know this: Dad was a lying, cheating, two-faced son-of-a-bitch," he snarled, vocal cords stretched to breaking. "He was A terrible husband and father and I don't want any part of celebrating him!"

Miles quivered with exasperation, gasping for air like a marathoner at the finish line. His chest ached, heart racing at a rabbit's pace. But he wasn't quite done. He looked Catherine square in the eye. "To be honest, I am glad he's dead. It'll be a relief to…"

Suddenly his head snapped abruptly to the right. The kitchen shattered into thousands of multi-colored shreds. His left cheek burned as if stung by a hundred hornets and his eye immediately puffed shut. *What the hell?* No, he quickly realized, the house hadn't blown up. Just his head. Then his still-open right eye caught a glint of light off the fake diamond ring on Catherine's right hand as it shot back from the opposite direction. The backhand raised a bookend welt on the right cheek.

"*I can't believe you hit me!* I am 30 years old! What is

wrong with you!?" His tongue tasted blood's unmistakable metallic tang on his swollen lower lip.

"Don't you ever talk about your father that way again!"

Miles couldn't believe his ears. "What? Are you crazy? After everything he did to you? My whole life I've listened to you complain about how bad your life was because of Dad, and now you're defending him?!"

Catherine grabbed his right wrist and her knife-like nails clawed into the fleshy underside. "How bad *my* life was – not yours! You are right. He was far from an ideal husband. But your father always loved you boys. He lived and breathed for *you*. Made sacrifices you can never begin to imagine or understand. He gave you a home and a name and a family. You criticize me for not taking responsibility for my choices, fine. But it's about time you grow up and understand what your father was before you criticize him for what he wasn't. Whatever he did to me, he deserved your respect in life, and he sure as hell deserves it in death!"

Catherine shook her head as if to clear her mind. "I need your help. I am asking for just one favor from you. I expect you to do this for me." Neither her suddenly smooth tone of voice nor calm demeanor invited or allowed further debate.

Miles realized his mouth hung open and snapped it shut. He jerked his arm back and discreetly rubbed the two crimson welts that had appeared on his wrist like a vampire's bite. He said nothing more, too stunned by all that had happened. Even if he could have found words, they probably couldn't have squeezed out of his swollen mouth.

Miles turned sharply and bolted from the kitchen to the foyer. He slid his feet into his shoes without bothering to tie the laces, bolted through the front door and slammed it. "Now that Dad's dead you might want to lock your goddamned door!" he yelled over his shoulder.

Standing on the porch, the painful ball of regret and guilt filling his gut, Miles heard the tinkle of breaking glass as an ornament plummeted from the shadow box.

12

A terrycloth tornado erupted inside the wet glass as the bartender slowly twisted the white towel.

Miles struggled to place the bartender's familiar face. A wave of déjà vu washed over him, yet he still couldn't figure out how he knew the man. He tried to disguise his confusion. Eyes darting from a chip in the mirror creating a tiny prism between bottles of cheap booze nestled against the glass behind the bartender, the mirror boxed by twinkling, colored lights – from Christmas maybe, but who knows how long they'd actually been there? – to the dark, wooden bar, lacquered with a lifetime of drunken spills. Then back again, discreetly catching the man's face a few seconds with each pass.

Professional basketball player tall, the bartender's clothes hung loosely on his lanky frame. Arms disproportionately long for the rest of his body, stubbed by hands that easily palmed and passed a dozen dirty glasses from a tray to the stainless-steel sink of sudsy water, then under a slow stream trickling from a faucet in the adjacent sink.

Long jaw…Unshaven cheeks…Disheveled, thinning hair…Still nothing. Miles squinted, trying to focus his memory. *How do I know you?* More glasses, more tornadoes.

The bar stool squeaked as Miles twisted, absent-minded, in half-circles. Suddenly, a bolt of recognition crackled.

"Larry! Larry Johnson!"

The bartender looked over. "Miles Ayala?" Miles knew he was right the second he heard that voice: an elastic, almost Southern drawl even more unique because Larry had never traveled farther south than Jordan, as far as Miles knew. That synthetic twang rang in Miles' ears for most of his pre-teen life. Larry's bony, spindly fingers clasped Miles' small hands and held on as if to a lifeline.

A smile wider than he had known in days creased Miles' face. "Yeah! Holy Christ, man, how long has it been?"

"Sheeeiitt… Thirteen years? Fifteen?"

"At least."

"Wow!" Larry said, releasing Miles' hand. "I can't believe it's you. What are you doin' in a dive like this on the East Side of Jordan?"

Miles' eyes swept his surroundings – which was probably more sweeping than it had seen in some time. Cold crept through the closed door like a drunk pining for a drink. The vent spewed an airborne cocktail of stale alcohol, cigarette smoke, piss, puke and something else he couldn't identify – sweat? shit? sex? The bitter mix scorched his eyes. An empty glass on the bar magnified a phone number carved into the wood for a woman who, the message promised, would make the caller very happy. Shoes stuck to the bare concrete floor, sucking and crackling as they lifted and dropped, step after step, toward the bar. Like the feet of a bug negotiating a fly strip in the summertime.

"Calling this place a dive is insulting to real dives." he said.

"Yer right about that. But it pays the bills. Well, at least some of 'em."

Anxious to change the subject, Miles said, "Hey, how's your mom doing?"

"She's moving slower now these days, but still kicking."

Funny…I didn't think she could move at all. Luckily, Miles' inner censor checked the immature, feeble attempt at humor. Larry's mother was a sweet-hearted, jovial, gentle single mother at a time when the world frowned on single parenthood. Her explosive laughter and the candy that she kept on hand for Larry's friends when they visited made it easy to like Angela Johnson. However, being what is now called "grossly obese," she was also an easy target for mocking among adolescent boys looking to carve some thin slice of superiority, even from a friend's innocent flesh. In his mind, Angela remained as she had been years ago, eternally perched on that high, brick porch. Dressed in clothes that looked poor even in their hand-me-down neighborhood. Gossiping with neighbors walking by as she kept a smiling eye on the neighborhood's activities. Her massive girth overflowing, yet miraculously contained by her nylon-stripped folding picnic chair. An acidic mix of shame and guilt sloshed in the pit of his stomach and Miles winced now at the cruelty he and the others had flung at Larry over his mother.

Incredibly, Larry seemed oblivious to anything but the present reality. "I thought y'all moved away a long time ago," Larry continued. "Westville, right?"

"I did." The smile abandoned his face. "My dad died last week so I had to come to town to talk to my mom about the arrangements."

"How'd you end up here?"

"You know, I didn't feel like going home yet. So, I drove around town for a while. Kind of zoned out. When I looked up, this was the first place I saw. So here I am. God works in funny ways…I had no idea you worked here, man. But it sure is nice to see a friendly face." *Now that I remember who you are…*

Sympathy replaced Larry's grin. "I'm so sorry to hear about your dad. He was a good guy."

Time's dam crumbled, and memories flooded the room. The boyhood friends reminisced as fast as they could pluck the memories from the thick, heavy air over their heads. Each story slightly embellished, the waters of time smoothing reality's sharper edges, glistening now with the sheen of history, easing the tension in Miles' head.

Endlessly exploring – but never quite solving – the torturous, inscrutable, life-altering mystery of Girls.

Trying out curse words – first tentative (and secret), sprinkling in a few "damns" or "shits" into a sentence here and there, then later, lobbing the F-bomb with the over-the-top confidence that comes with early unbridled adolescence.

Riding bikes for hours, miles away from home. Who cared? No one was concerned about weirdoes hurting kids in *those* days.

"Remember playing Hide and Seek until it was so dark you didn't need to really hide, 'cause no one was going to find you anyway?"

"How about swimmin' all day in your pool?" Larry drawled. "Dive bombin' each other off that rickety deck yer dad built? Shoot, man, it's a miracle no one was ever killed!!"

"Or playing baseball in the yard? How many times did we hit foul balls and break my aunt's window?"

"God, man! How about that time your dad took us all on that hike to the old paper mill so that we could" – Larry's eyes lit up; his voice deepened with an affected, melodramatic tone – "FIND FRANKENSTEIN!"

Miles erupted with laughter.

Larry planted his bony hands on the bar and took one step back, stretching and bending his lanky frame. "He'd pretend like he heard somethin', and then let us shoot his police guns into the woods. Lord, I cannot believe we didn't get in any trouble for that."

"Well then you didn't know my dad very well." Miles shot a sharp gaze at Larry. "No one messed with the Great Michael Ayala." Miles heard the sarcasm and cynicism in his voice and wondered if Larry had noticed. He tried to change the subject without Larry noticing.

"You're looking good my friend. About the same as I remember you."

"Well, shooooot…That's mighty nice of you, but I know it ain't true! I wish I could say the same for you."

As if he'd been hit in the head, Miles sat momentarily stunned by the blunt response. Of course, Larry'd never been one to acknowledge much less stand on ceremony.

"Hey man, I don't mean to hurt your feelin's or nothin'. I'm just sayin', you look like you been beat all to hell and back."

Miles caught his reflection in the bar mirror. Larry was right. Sunken cheeks. Flat, dull eyes. Tight lips, corners drooping under some invisible weight. Grayer than he remembered. Certainly, more than a thirty-year-old man should have. "Man, you're right. I guess the strain of the last few days and all…" Miles added, trying to navigate the turn the conversation had taken. "Ah well, what the hell…Since I am here, I may as well have a drink or two."

"Of course. What do you want?"

"Jack Daniels, straight."

"You're a whiskey man, huh?"

"Yeah. My best college buddy's wife recently turned me on to it. Schooling me on all the finer points, which ones to try, what makes one better than the other. You know, like that."

"Most women prefer wine to the harder stuff," Larry observed.

"True, but she's not most women. Gorgeous, smart, and tough. I love her to death. She's perfect for my friend. He likes to act all gruff, but she sees through all that crap. He's really a softie. It's hilarious to see them together. She matches him step for step, doesn't take any of his nonsense. She keeps him in line." Smiling, he raised the glass to eye level, peering deeply into the glass as if The Meaning of Life – or more likely in this joint, a bug – floated in its amber contents. "Anyway, I been doing a lot of my own 'research' the last few days, if you know what I mean," Miles said. "Here's to…What should we toast?"

"How about your dad?"

Miles didn't have the energy to detail his mental manifesto of grievances against his father. He opted for an easier answer. "Nah. Too obvious. How about this?" Miles extended his left hand across the bar and clasped Larry's emaciated wrist. "Here's to a bridge of friendship stretching across fifteen long years."

"You OK?"

Miles swirled the cubes in his glass, now melding into the amber liquid. "You have time to talk?"

Larry's head swiveled left, then right. The bar stood empty save for the two of them and a disheveled woman who looked like she'd taken root in a corner booth. She was vigorously arguing with herself and clearly wasn't going anywhere soon. "Time ain't a problem here, buddy," Larry said. "How much time you need?

He tipped the glass toward his friend, once long-lost, now miraculously found, then returned it to his pursed lips. He drained the liquid fire in one unbroken motion, savoring its slow, cleansing burn all the way to the bottom of his troubled spirit.

13

So many unfamiliar hands…unrecognized faces…implausible stories…shaking, smiling, speaking…a frothing whirlpool of anxiety and aggravation…

Miles peered over the shoulder of the mourner in front of him to the back of the funeral home. The line of well-wishers hadn't diminished as he'd hoped. It had grown. Now another one presented himself.

Who was this man who'd introduced himself only minutes before? He'd hardly heard a word the poor guy had said. Or any of them, for that matter. Cops. Lawyers. Family. Friends. A couple women no one seemed to know. An informant who was the spitting image of Charles Manson. Even a recently-released convict – probably just to make sure Michael had really died. Expressing condolences, sharing memories, singing his praises. Yet Miles knew that the words were just different notes in the same flat, tiresome, repetitious tune:

"I knew Mikey when he was little..."
"Oh, your dad was such a wonderful man..."
"We grew up in the old neighborhood..."
"He helped me when my..."

As the oldest son, Miles was the second-to-the-last of Michael's immediate family to receive well-wishers. First, the baby, Benjie and his bride of a year; then Parker and his wife; then Maya; then himself; before finishing the Michael Ayala Condolences Tour with Catherine.

Miles could hardly hear any of the visitors over the caterwauling shrieks of the female Ayala relatives commandeering the row of seats nearest the casket.

His tired eyes ached from the lighting – dimmed to soften the room, but so low that it was hard to see anything more than a few feet away without squinting.

The smell of the funeral flowers assaulted his nose the second he entered the parlor. The perfume from the veritable floral mausoleum guarding the casket – ribboned and festooned wreaths, baskets, plants and arrangements of orchids, lilies, roses and carnations – mixed with the chemical odor of cleaning products, on top of a subtle hint of what Miles would later swear was embalming fluid.

His head throbbed from the sensorial beating, his stomach turned queasy somersaults and his legs felt like he'd just run a thousand-mile marathon.

He leaned slightly to his right. "Mom, how much longer?"

"What?" Catherine said.

"When can we can take a break?" Miles whispered as a mourner stopped the procession to share yet another anecdote with Parker. "It feels like we've been here forever. I'm tired and hungry."

"Are you serious?" Catherine hissed through a plastic smile into the space between them without turning her head to avoid drawing attention. Her tight, parental voice was barely audible – yet he felt like she'd clubbed him over the head. "We've only been here for an hour. You will stay here with me until we are done, I don't care how long it takes. You are a man, not a little boy and you have adult responsibilities. Grow up!"

Miles flinched at his mother's cutting tone, then straightened. Always the dutiful son.

Suddenly, his head swiveled toward the phrase that would likely devour today, and many tomorrows: "I'm so sorry for your loss," said yet another middle-aged man that Miles did not recognize.

"Thank you." Miles mechanically shook the man's cold, leathery hand. He held the courtesy gesture as long as possible to check every detail – clothing, facial hair, speech pattern, accent – searching desperately for a clue. Something to place him in familiar context. Miles reddened with each passing second, embarrassed about his flailing memory.

Finally, he admitted defeat, exasperated both with himself and the situation which had repeated several times already. "I'm so sorry, I don't remember your name." Miles tried to laugh off his frustration with a standby self-deprecation. "It's the great curse of my professional life – ten years as a newspaper reporter, but I am still terrible with names."

The visitor kindly rescued Miles. "Judge Pokorny. Your dad appeared before me in my courtroom many times over the years when he was with the Sheriff's department."

"Ah!" Miles said, pretending that a light had just illuminated a dark corner of his memory. *Well, at least I couldn't have been reasonably expected to know this one...*

"Please don't worry about it, young man, I understand. You and your family have a lot on your plates today. I'm not sure anyone could do any better under the circumstances. I mean, look at that line!" He tossed his head toward the back of the room. "That's why I came early. I know a lot of people loved and admired your dad, but I can't believe how many people are here. I think I was number forty-eight in the registry and there must be three hundred people waiting already."

Pokorny's words struck Miles like lightning and squeezed his chest...like one of those "Indian burns" that Parker used to give, grabbing and twisting Miles' forearm as if wringing out a washcloth. He still bore bruises (psychic, if not actually physical) from the years of torture his younger, but much larger brother had doled while growing up. Miles may have been older, smarter. But Parker was bigger, and he never had a qualm about using his size to bully Miles. To this day, Miles hated him for it. *The fat fuck...*

He dropped Pokorny's hand as if he'd grabbed a live wire.

112

"Well, umm, thank you very much for coming," he stammered, uncharacteristically. "We, uh, er, I mean, we appreciate it very much." Miles looked toward Catherine, who was still visiting with another mourner. "I am very sure my mom will want to talk to you ve..." He clutched, realizing he'd almost said "very much" three times in a row, and changed course. "I mean, a lot." Laying his hand on Pokorny's shoulder, Miles gently guided the judge over to Catherine – and away from himself.

"Mom, this is Judge Pokorny. He worked with dad for a long time."

Catherine smoothly took Pokorny's hand like they were lifelong friends. "Well of course! Hi Mark – I mean, *Your Honor.* How are you?" She flashed a broad smile.

Jesus Christ, is she flirting with him?

"No, Mark is fine, Catherine," Pokorny said, returning her smile. "I was so sorry to hear about Michael. You know he was a wonderful deputy and detective. One of the few I really respected from the bench, and I cannot say that about many of the cops who come into my courtroom. Did you ever hear about the time that he..."?

Miles turned away. Their voices trailed off. Miles didn't have to hear the words. He knew that Pokorny was sharing one more story to cement the wall of Michael Ayala Lore being built that morning, one fake, phony, ignorant brick at a time.

Only an hour into eight – and eight more tomorrow – and already, the wall was higher than Miles believed it could be – or knew it should be.

Look at her! Devouring every goddamned word. Thanking everyone like they just threw her a lifeline instead of drowning her in lies. Suddenly he froze. Snapped around, military-style.

Stepped toward his mother and the judge.

"Excuse me, sir…" Miles interrupted.

He caught Catherine's gaze, staring deep into her eyes, hoping that somehow, she'd comprehend his suffering. Why he couldn't stand here one second more. Why he needed to just get the hell out of there for a few minutes.

Catch his breath.

Ease the pressure in his chest.

Rearrange his mental furniture.

He had hoped she'd understand and forgive, but he'd settle for understanding.

"Mom," he gently took her hand and spoke slower than necessary, as if speaking in code. "I need some air. I'll be back soon."

Catherine's eyes tapered to daggers. Her well-maintained nails dug into his palm. "Ok, honey, get some water or a bite to eat and come on back quickly."

His whole life, this had been her way to privately express displeasure with stiletto-like clarity in public. Usually the tactic earned a wince, at least.

But not this time.

In fact, Miles decided, never again.

He withdrew his reddened palm, turned and shook Pokorny's hand. Later, Miles thought maybe the shake had been a little too enthusiastic given the circumstances. "Judge, thanks again for coming. We appreciate your condolences."

Miles then took Catherine's hand again and quickly and harshly squeezed her fingers between his. She gasped. Pokorny turned toward them.

Miles narrowed his own gaze.

Smiled at Catherine.

Held the crushing grip.

Drew out his words, laboring over each syllable. Making his point as clearly and painfully as she had made hers.

"I will come back," he said almost jovially, squeezing even harder. "As. Soon. As. Possible."

14

Head pounding, knees quivering, Miles clung to the back of a chair in the funeral home's guest room.

He stared at the mismatched mish-mosh of half-eaten munchies, picked-over sandwiches, sampled salsas and dips (half a chip emerged from the center of one, like a shark's fin), cakes missing random slices, cookies stacked haphazardly on plates around the room, a pan of lasagna, a plate of tamales, more breads than a bakery display case...

Miles weighed his hunger against the likelihood of contracting food poisoning by eating any of this stuff that had been open, unrefrigerated, since early this morning. A wave of nausea burbled up his throat, ending that debate. He gripped the chair harder, struggling to steady himself. Eyes closed, head lowered, trying to slow the room's spin.

Airy wisps of condolences and comments floated across the hallway from the main parlor where Catherine, his brothers and Maya continued receiving well-wishers.

A watery whooshing ebbed and crashed in his ears. He didn't know the cause – whether the unyielding soupy noise or the whiskey-provoked ache inside his skull that even the eight Ibuprofen he'd slammed that morning couldn't ease. Regardless, the pain competed for space in his head with the words that had been swimming there for days...*Hurts too much...Can't do it...I can't...*

"Can't do what? I'm surprised you can even stand up!"

Miles didn't realize he'd spoken the words. He gingerly turned his head. Benjie, Miles' youngest sibling, smiled from the doorway. He stepped into the room and reached his oldest brother in two steps, simultaneously propping him up as he began lightly massaging his shoulders. The pain began releasing. A universe became a supernova behind Miles' eyes. "Oh my god, that feels so good, Benjie. Sorry I had to bail there. I needed a few minutes to catch my breath."

"You don't need to explain or apologize. I understand. You still look a little green around the gills."

"Man, Crayola would have to invent a new shade of green for how I feel right now." Miles quietly accepted this moment of grace as Benjie's hands did their best to untie the knots in his neck and shoulders. "I can't remember if I thanked you for coming to get me last night. I was in no shape to drive."

"No problem, big brother. I'm happy you called. Frankly, you were in no shape to drive, ride, run, walk or crawl!"

Miles stared at his littlest brother with eyes clouded as much by his roiling nausea as laughter at Benjie's innocent, gentle poke. Benjie often needled his brothers. Biting humor often was the only weapon he had in their sibling hierarchy. Miles was the oldest. Parker the biggest. His eternal status as The Baby wasn't much in the scheme of things, but it had earned him a disproportionate degree of latitude – certainly more than Miles normally gave anyone else. "I don't doubt that one bit. But I still can't believe you came all the way across town to pick me up."

"Seriously, you know I don't mind."

"Well, in any case, thank you. I truly don't know why you are so nice to me," Miles said.

Benjie continued his massage. "C'mon, it's what brothers do. I know you'd do the same for me if the puke was on the other shoe!"

Miles struggled to stifle a laugh, not wanting to antagonize the throbbing pain in his head. "Please, don't make jokes. And don't be so sure I would have done the same for you. Just because we're related doesn't mean I have to like you or be nice to you. Mom and Dad made it very clear when you were born – we only had to tolerate you and try not to kill you. I mean, Parker and I were fine all by ourselves for five glorious years. And then, wham! *You* came along."

The sentiment had been shared so often it took on the shape of a joke, but the guilt that stabbed his heart testified to its truth. Facts were facts, no matter how much humor was lacquered over them. For most of their adolescence, Miles and Parker were inseparable. Only 16 months apart, they were raised –and thought of – as virtual twins, a condition they very much capitalized on in school, with friends and activities and social interests. But, Benjie, if he was thought of at all, was always just…The Baby. That Other One. The third wheel rolling clumsily alongside him and Parker wherever they went.

Sometimes in the most jealousy-dusted corners of his mind, Miles thought of Benjie as something else. Something even worse. He was Michael and Catherine's "real" child.

"Truth be told, I never liked you growing up. You were a snot-nosed little brat who always got whatever you wanted because you were 'The Baby.' I remember Mom always telling me and Parker to include you, play with you, take you places. *He's just a baby. He doesn't have any friends his own age. He wants to be big like you two.'* Jesus, I hated that crap."

"Hey, I understand! I felt the same way about you and Parker. For most of my life, you two were just the big jerks who slept in the room across the hall who were always being mean to me," Benjie shot back.

"Mean to you?" Wide-eyed and smiling, Miles feigned innocence. "Us?"

Another smile eased the tension in the air. "And I resented Mom's interference too. I had plenty of friends. They weren't your friends, but then we were five years apart, so why would anyone expect us to have the same friends or do the same things? But look at us now! Time has a way of making things better, I think."

True enough, Miles thought. Defined by a deceptive intelligence, wickedly sharp humor and deep (though often hard to see, from the surface) pools of empathy, Benjie had become an adult he respected, relied on, and even admired. He and Benjie had grown closer as the distance increased between he and Parker as Parker had made his way along a path Miles couldn't quite understand, defend or approve.

Benjie released his magical grip. "Ugh, don't stop!" Miles pleaded before collapsing into the chair he'd been leaning on. He rubbed his temples and watched in not-totally-fake horror as Benjie scouted the snacks. Tall, wiry and muscular like their father, with Michael's same olive-tinted skin tone – Michael appeared more Greek or Italian than Hispanic (his young, single mother never confirmed his true paternity before she died in an accident, creating an ongoing family mystery) mischievous eyes and an easy, sly laugh, like he always knew the punchline before you even heard the joke, Benjie had always been as easy on the eyes as we he was on the soul. But Miles noted a thickening layer of "baby fat" on his baby brother as he edged toward the back end of his twenties. As a kid, Benjie had always been a persnickety eater, shying away from salads and anything else that might pass for healthy. Now, he plated two tamales, a chunk of rubbery macaroni and cheese, a tower of tortilla chips, a mound of refried beans, coleslaw as big as the head of cabbage that produced it, and a pile of homemade Spanish rice. For good measure, he blanketed the entire culinary offense in hot salsa. Cutting a large slice of chocolate chip cheesecake, he turned back to Miles.

"You want something?" He waved his plate toward his brother.

"Good God, no. How can you eat *anything*?" Miles' stomach churned again.

Benjie plopped into the chair across from Miles and barely raised his eyes from the mountainous fare. The baby brother shoveled several forkfuls into his mouth.

*Whatever...*Miles thought, uninterested in debating the dietary disaster happening only three feet away. "I can't go back in there," he said, shaking his head slowly, his eyes gray with exhaustion and fatigue.

"What do you mean?" he mumbled around the half-chewed food.

"I mean I can't go back in there. I am tired of mom's bullshit – smiling that fake smile at everyone like nothing is wrong. Listening to everyone sing dad's praises. Not to mention that I feel like I'm going to throw up every ten minutes..."

Benjie finally stopped eating. He licked his fingers.

"That is so disgusting!" Miles scolded. "Use a napkin for Chris' sakes!"

Benjie glared at Miles.

"No, that's not disgusting." The words fell slowly, like crumbs from Benjie's lips. "What's disgusting, and really sad, is you continuing to feel so sorry for yourself."

For the first time in nearly twenty-four hours, Miles' head was suddenly clear. "What'd you say?"

"You heard me. You're acting like a complete and total dick." Benjie crammed another crust of apple pie into his mouth.

Is that spinach dip on that pie? Miles shuddered. "You don't know what you're talking about. You have no idea what I'm feeling."

"No, actually I do," Benjie said, gnawing on a mound of reddened pasta. "Everyone – and I mean, everyone – in the family knows how you feel, and that you don't want to do the eulogy, because you won't shut the hell up about it! Parker, Grandma, Maya, even Mom."

Benjie wedged a handful of what appeared to be plain wheat crackers into his bulging cheeks. "And we're all sick of hearing about it."

"Are you kidding me?" Miles wobbled as he tried to stand up, but the swirling nausea, still outweighing his indignation and anger, forced him back into the chair. "Mom only wants me to do the eulogy because she's too lazy to do it and doesn't want to be bothered. She has no consideration for my feelings."

"Oh my god! Would you give it up please?!" He finally stopped eating and shoved the nearly empty plate across the table toward Miles. "I have never heard so much self-pity from any *three* people! You know, for someone so smart you sure are stupid sometimes. *Yes*, Mom wants you to do the eulogy. Why wouldn't she? You're the best writer and talker in our family. You could make the phone book sound like an Oscar-winning movie. That's a good thing, you asshole! It'll make her life just a little bit easier right now. That's also a good thing. She needs someone to lean on now. You're the oldest, so that's your job. And if you weren't so busy feeling sorry for yourself like a bitch, you'd see that!"

"Did you call me a bitch, you son-of-a-bitch?" This time, Miles made it to his feet – slow, feeble, wobbling, but standing.

"Yeah I did!" Benjie too now stood, the front of his shirt a greasy mosaic of dribbled sauces and food scraps. "What are you going to do about it? Hit me? You can barely walk, you're so hung over! Maybe I should have left you in that shithole last night. At least you would've blended right in with all the other drunks and losers!" Benjie snarled. "If my dad was here right now, he'd beat your ass!"

My dad?

The words hung there for several seconds, hovering between Miles and Benjie like tiny, bomb-wielding hummingbirds.

Of course, Miles had thought as much himself countless times. Wondering about, debating, questioning his relationship to the man who had not helped conceive him, but had given him a life, nonetheless. Was he, Miles, truly Michael Ayala's son in some way more than name? And if he wasn't Michael Ayala's blood son, what did that make him? The answer was as clear to Miles as it was shameful: an orphan of the worst kind. A bastard in the eyes of the world around him that could see so clearly that he looked nothing like the man who'd injected himself into the life of a helpless, desperate single mother so that he could selfishly call himself Father.

Still, it was one thing for Miles to question his relationship with his dad. It was quite another for someone – anyone – and especially his baby brother to raise the issue. Were the words an innocent Freudian slip? Perhaps. A teasing, brotherly stab at a button that Benjie had learned how to push over the years as a defense mechanism? Maybe. And in a different time, Miles might have been more willing to let them evaporate, unacknowledged. And he answered Benjie as his faith-filled heart had always answered his own doubtful mind.

But, not today.

Today, the green of envy replaced the green of nausea.

"Your dad? *Your* dad!"

"Wait." Benjie held up his hands, palm out, in a gesture of subservient surrender. "I didn't mean it that way. You know I didn't. You're my big brothers. I don't always like you guys, but I love both of you."

"Don't give me that lovey-dovey crap! The mouth is the window to your heart!"

Benjie burped an unintentional half chuckle. "What does that even *mean*?"

"It means that you said exactly what you meant!" Miles yelled, showing no signs of ending this rant any time soon.

"I swear, it was a Freudian slip, man, I promise. I didn't mean anything by it." Benjie lowered his voice, slowed his pace, trying to defuse the drunken time bomb that threatened to explode – verbally and literally across the table from him. "Calm down before you really do get sick."

"Bullshit!" Miles seethed, panting with the effort of keeping his balance, wiping spit from the corner of his mouth. "You have always told people that *you* were Dad's *real* son. Admit it!"

"I never said that. And if I did, it was on accident. Not on purpose!"

Miles wobbled, his eyes glazing from the cocktail of anger, exhaustion and alcohol. His words started to bump into and roll over each other, like waves approaching and departing the same place on the shore. "You always thought you were thought you were better than Parker and me. You could do no wrong." he sneered. "The *golden child!*"

"C'mon man, slow down. Take a breath. Think about what you're saying. You're hung over." Benjie shuffled his feet slightly, positioning himself to catch Miles if – or more likely, when – he toppled.

"I may be hung over, but I can still talk well enough to tell you that he was as much my dad and Parker's dad as he was yours! Maybe even more! He *chose* to adopt us!"

"I know that!" Benjie insisted. "Please stop. People are staring!

"Fuck them," Miles said loud enough to be heard in the next room, then at the top of his voice, "and *fuck you!* For all anyone knows, *you* were an accident, you asshole!"

Miles lunged for Benjie. His baby brother – younger sprier, and sober – easily dodged the attack. Miles grasped at empty air, stumbling, tumbling onto the table.

He landed, face down, panting, sprawled squarely on the mole hill remnants of Benjie's former food mountain. Miles crinkled his nose as the acrid remnants of last night's whiskey rose from the back of his throat and escaped his lips, burning his nostrils as it wafted between his nose hairs.

"Hey!"

Miles and Benjie turned to see an attractive, dark-complexioned middle-aged woman in the lounge doorway. Though she partially blocked their view, Miles could see faces over her shoulder in the reception area turning toward the ruckus.

Miles liked and loved, to varying degrees all his Ayala relatives – "relative" being a relative term, given his and Parker's adoption and the Ayala clan's confoundingly-loose definition of Family. Yet, no matter the semantics or bloodline, Carmen Munoz was, by far, Miles' favorite aunt on his dad's side. Throughout his childhood and especially his adolescence, she'd been friend, confidant, protector, mentor – even mother, on a few occasions. When he thought of her – always fondly – he saw the radiant, toothy smile and heard her full-throated, high pitched laugh that crackled as if the joy it conveyed was too big to contain.

Aunt Carmen neither smiled nor laughed now.

"The two of youse, stop this right now!" she ordered. "Your dad would be ashamed of both of you!"

Miles' head swiveled slowly. He locked eyes with Benjie and snarled under his breath.

"See? I told you…*our* dad."

Benjie's eyes rolled. "That's what I've been saying all along."

<u>15</u>

"Sit." Carmen commanded.

Miles hesitated. "I don't want to sit…"

"I wasn't asking. Sit!"

Miles stood for a few seconds more, reluctant to line up for the inevitable tongue lashing. Finally, he slowly dragged a metal folding chair across the room, its rubber-tipped feet squawking in protest. He dropped heavily into the chair across the table from his aunt, hoping against hope that she remembered she was his favorite – and that she held him in equally high regard (as he secretly believed). He figured her grace-filled love, patience and understanding was his only hope for salvation.

"Look at me," she ordered.

He could not look in her eyes. Instead he peered over her shoulder toward the main parlor where Parker and Benjie struggled to contain Catherine. If looks could kill, Miles would be laying in that coffin next to his dad…

"I said, *look at me,* Miles Ayala." She sounded more like his mother than like his favorite aunt. He picked a few black olive slices from the Dali-like smear of food on his tie and shirt.

"I can't." Miles continued staring into his lap, unable to hoist the weight of his chin.

"Why not?"

"I don't know."

"Yes, you do," Carmen insisted.

"Because I'm ashamed of myself."

Now, he cautiously raised his eyes to meet hers. He hoped his blooming mortification would serve as a small act of contrition and appease the twin demons of disappointment and remorse gnawing on his guts. However, Carmen's face showed no sign of clemency. An angry scowl supplanted her usual smile. *Not good…* His silent prayer for forgiveness quickly became simple gratitude that, at the very least, bolts of lightning did not shoot from her eyes and vaporize him on the spot.

"You *should* be ashamed of yourself." Carmen's sharp, authoritarian tone shocked Miles. She had never reprimanded him – not that he'd ever given her much reason, being the "good one" among Michael's three sons. "I have never seen such a display from you – or any adult for that matter. My five-year-old granddaughter has never thrown such a tantrum!"

Another log of guilt landed on the blazing pyre consuming his soul…

"Miles, you know I love you…" Her voice softened a

bit.

Thank God…

"…but what has gotten into you? What in the world is going on? You embarrassed your mother, your wife, your brothers, and me, too."

All true, affirmed by the stunned stares still floating across the hallway from many of the mourners. These wounds hurt, but they would heal, Miles assured himself, taking a tentative step toward self-absolution.

But Carmen had saved her harshest shot for last.

"If your dad was here, he would have killed you!"

The lingering effects of the previous night's lost battle with the whiskey bottle dulled Miles' judgment and sense of irony. Still, he knew enough to not dare argue with or even try to make light of his aunt's amusing, but twisted logic.

"Benjie and I just had a little disagreement." He attempted a conciliatory half-grin to test the depths of Carmen's anger.

"First of all, don't mess with me, Miles! This is no joke. Look at this mess! I cannot believe I saw what I just saw. You can thank your lucky stars I'm not your mother. Because if I was? Well, you'd be sorry, I can tell you! Second, you know exactly what I mean. *What. Is. Wrong. With. You?*" She hammered each word like nails, each strike harder, louder than the last.

Cornered like a lowly rat and unsure how much of his aunt's good will he'd burned through Miles meekly began offering his standard response about not wanting to do his dad's eulogy.

Carmen indulged his self-pity for half a minute, then

cut him off.

"That's a bunch of nonsense and you know it!" His aunt had never spoken to him so angrily. Her unfamiliar tone stung as if she'd slapped his face.

"What? You asked what's wrong with me, and I'm telling you."

"No, you're just making an excuse for feeling sorry for yourself. You just feel guilty for treating your mom so bad and disrespecting your father."

"Me? Treating *her* bad?"

"Yes."

Miles eyes squinted in disbelief and defiance. "Do you even know what you're saying? Do you know how awful she has been since dad died? How mean and hateful and vengeful she's been my entire life? You have no idea what she says about you. How she hates all of the Ayalas because you wouldn't let go of your precious 'Mikey'." Miles realized he crossed a line. He clamped his mouth shut, anticipating an angry flood of criticism.

Instead, Carmen responded calmly. Her peaceful, reasonable tone was unexpected given the revelations he'd just shared, yet predictable for the kind soul she embodied. She nudged some food toward the middle of the table to make room, leaned forward on her elbows, her arms flat, hands neatly clasped.

"Sweetheart, you are one of the brightest people I know. I am so proud of you for who you are and the young man you have become. You're a kind, thoughtful person, you take care of everyone – Maya, your kids, me, our family. Even your mom. You are so talented, and good looking (she winked – their private joke and bond since he came into the family as a little boy). And you're so smart. Smarter than almost anyone I know…"

Her kind words soothed his tired heart and throbbing head. Alas, he assumed détente too quickly.

"That's why I am so irritated with you right now. I don't understand why *you* don't understand what's really going on here."

"What?" Miles recoiled, confused.

"Of course, I know what your mom says about us. I've known your mom for more than thirty years now. Trust me, I don't always like her either. A lot of the times, I just tolerated her. We all did. That's not the point. The point is, I did it because I *know* her. I understand why she feels the way she does and says what she says."

"Oh, please!" Miles pushed back. "I have heard all the 'Catherine Stories' about how hard her childhood was, how no one liked her, she was treated like a built-in babysitter for her brothers and sisters, and how she married my biological father to get out of the house and married dad for Parker and me."

"But honey, that's the point. They're not just stories. If they were, I wouldn't put up with her. No one would. Yes, she can be difficult. She talks and behaves that way because she's been hurt, too, and a lot of that hurt came from her marriage to your dad – both of them. It's not a good excuse, I know. She should know better and act better. She says mean things. She says things in a mean way. But she's not a mean *person*. And, believe it or not she's not lying. I know your mom better than you think. Even better than maybe she thinks."

"So, what? She's some kind of hero now?"

Carmen filtered a laugh through a wry grin. "No, I would never say that. Not by a longshot. Your mom has hurt too many people over the years to say that, including me," she said.

"But I am saying that she is a special person. She's spent her entire life taking care of everyone around her. First it was her brothers and sisters, then it was her kids, then both of her husbands, without getting a whole lot back in return except for a lot of grief and hard times. She's just trying to take care of your dad, one last time. That's not saying a lot, I guess, but it's saying something that needs to be said, and that your mom deserves," Carmen said. "That doesn't make her a hero, or even unique, really. That just makes her a mother and a wife. That's what women do, at least women of our generation." Carmen pointed a perfectly manicured index finger at Miles. "Which is something no man – including you – can ever understand."

Miles paused as Carmen's words floated in front of his eyes. What she said made sense, but he wasn't ready to give up the fight.

"Fine. If you know so much about her, then you also know how badly dad treated her. The constant teasing in front of people. The cheating. The physical and emotional abuse. He might have been a great cop and a good father, but he was a lousy husband! I was *there*, Carmen. I know! No matter how crazy or mean mom might be, she didn't deserve to be treated that way by anyone, much less her husband! And now she wants me to say nice things about him? No way!"

He breathed deeply to slow his racing heart, then pushed himself back from the table to leave.

"Honey, I do know. All of it. And probably even more."

Stunned, Miles dropped back into the chair. His tongue felt like a fish flopping in a net. "What? You knew? Then why…how…"

"For the same reason as your mom. I do not, I mean, *did* not always like your dad, but I know him. I know who he was. Yes, your dad could be terrible, too. He was like that to a lot of people. Including me. What he thought was funny or ok could be incredibly mean and hurtful," Carmen said. "But I also know who he was trying to be. And when he was *that* person, he could also be a wonderful man."

Feeling his face twisting into a pretzel of red disgust, Miles started to respond – "How can you say that? He was a terrible…"

"Yes, he *could be* terrible," Carmen interjected, "but he could also be wonderful. Honey, he was human. Bad and good, just like the rest of us. Think of everything he did for you and Parker. Everything he gave you."

"Like what?"

Carmen reached across the table and gently took Miles' hands into her own. "Well, your name to start with, and a family who loves you very much. He gave you a different world." Miles had to admit, he loved everything else about his adoptive culture. The food, the music, the language, the literature. So much so, that when people questioned his heritage, confused by the clash between his white skin and "brown" surname he'd proudly say he was half Mexican "by association," rather than by blood.

"Most of all, even though he didn't show it all the time, your dad loved your mom when she needed it most," Carmen said.

Miles dropped his head, resigned to a truth he couldn't deny.

"I really think that's why you're so hurt and upset," Carmen continued, her thumbs softly stroking the backs of Miles' hands. "You loved your dad very much when he was here. Too much to hate him now that he's gone.

"But he hurt my mom so bad," Miles said, softly lobbing his one firm battle cry again.

"True. But believe it or not, she loved him. I was there when they got married and he adopted you. For a while, they really did love each other. They were young, they created a new family together, starting with two beautiful sons."

"And what did he give her besides misery?"

"What every woman wanted. At least, every woman back then. I know it's hard for your generation to understand this, but women our age, we defined ourselves by our husbands, our children. We didn't have big careers outside the home. Our *home* was our career."

A drop of clarity formed quickly on Miles' face then evaporated in a flash, leaving a frown where a smile had briefly been.

"Look, death shows us for who we really are, and it's usually not very pretty. You're punishing your dad, and your mom, too, for not being perfect instead of appreciating them for being what they were. Good, loving people with flaws like the rest of us. That's human. Understandable. They both made huge sacrifices for each other, and for you boys."

"I understand, I really do, but what's that got to do with me doing his eulogy?"

"Because you and your mom did the same thing, but in reverse. You saw your dad on a pedestal your whole life, and then you were disappointed when he kept falling off. She kept putting him up onto the pedestal and got angry when he wouldn't stay there."

"Look, don't take this the wrong way, but would you please speak English?" Miles said, unable to hide his exasperation with his aunt's verbal gymnastics. "Why would she try to make him look like a better person than he really was?"

Carmen smiled for the first time since they'd sat down. "Sometimes I cannot believe how dumb you men are. If *he* looked better, then *she* looked better by association. If he was a 'success'– a good man, a good father, a good husband – then she could say she was, too. When everything was 'right' with your dad, then everything was right in their family, and *her family was her world*."

Shocked, Miles straightened in his chair. That thought had never occurred to him.

"More important, she did it to justify choosing him to be your father. She didn't have to, you know. Your mom was so pretty when she was young. She could have had anyone she wanted. And she chose your dad. Don't get me wrong, he was quite a catch himself. Dark, handsome, great smile, funny. If he wasn't my cousin, I might even say sexy!" Carmen chuckled. "Of course, your dad knew all of that about himself, too, which was a big part of his problem. He was always adorable, cute, charming – not to mention the baby in the family – so everyone always let him get away with murder. As awful as he could be, at least it was usually behind closed doors. Now, imagine how bad it would look if people knew your mom chose such a flawed man to raise her children? She spent their married life together trying to make him perfect. Now, do you see?"

Miles nodded slowly, the fog of confusion replaced by thickening clouds of guilt. "Why didn't she just marry someone who would have loved *her* more and made *her* happy?" he nearly whispered.

"Listen Miles, as much as she's mad at the family now, your mom and I are actually pretty close, and believe me, I asked your mom the same thing a thousand times over the years. Every time she called me late at night, crying because they had a fight, or he had hit her or said something terrible. She always said the same thing. 'Because he loves the boys.'"

His chest caved again under a new wave of remorse.

"You may not want to believe it. You may even resent her for it, but she truly did marry your dad for you and your brother. She hoped if you and Parker were happy, and Michael was happy, then she would be happy too."

Silence now flooded the room which, only minutes ago, had exploded with noisy fury. Miles remembered, not for the first time, how much he loved this woman though they shared nothing but a name. He stared, wordless, at his aunt. Finally, he exhaled, emptying his body of springs of anxiety and tension.

"Your mom needs you to put him back on that pedestal. For his sake, for your sake, and yes, for hers. She can't do it herself. Everything is still too raw and close for her. Parker can't do it. He idolizes your dad. And Benjie cannot speak to any of this. Now don't be mad at me for saying this, but he is Michael's blood child." Miles cringed at the undeniable logic of her assessment.

"But you are his oldest son. You were the first. In a lot of ways, you're the best. You're the only one who can tell the truth about your dad without hurting him. Or, her."

"Ok. I'll do it, but only because you asked." Plus, Miles knew, any speech is a chance to perform. Even a eulogy. Like any preacher or musician, Miles loved the electrified thrill of conducting an audience. Taking them on an emotional roller coaster, propelled by his well-chosen words, juicing their emotions, then bringing them down to earth for a safe rhetorical landing. And, arrogant as it sounds, Miles wasn't ashamed to say he was damn good at it, too.

He stood and stepped toward Carmen to hug her, then slipped on a rogue dollop of guacamole and crashed to the floor.

"Oh, honey! Are you alright? Let me help you." Carmen reached down to him up.

He rose, took shelter in her open arms, clinging to the only thing that felt real – the only thing that had made any sense – since Michael had died.

The thought rolled through, leading a wash of gratitude.

You already have.

16

Miles slammed the car door so hard the window rattled, triggering a mini avalanche from the top of the car.

Little snow-filled cyclones skittered across the parking lot and blanketed his car hood with a thickening layer of wet flakes. He remembered the weatherman predicting a bit of snow today but didn't think it would be this much. Miles was a competent – if not entirely confident – driver. Yet this kind of weather made him anxious, what with six winter fender benders (though only two were his fault, really, Miles assured himself).

He didn't know what angered him more – Maya refusing to ride home with him because of his "tantrum" (as she called it), or his mother getting the best of him. Either way, it would be a long, silent drive on a cold January night.

Once again, she pushes every one of my buttons and makes me look like a fool in front of God and everybody. As usual, she never takes any responsibility for her own behavior…never understands that she's as much to blame as Dad…that she made her own choices and her own life!

The day's unfortunate events replayed in his mind. Shame swelled his throat. Sighing, he turned the key and adjusted the heating vents as the car purred to life. He ripped out of the parking lot but eased off the gas pedal when the car skidded a bit. The day had been bad enough. Now, the evening offered no relief. His hands clamped around the steering wheel, positioned precisely at ten and two like it was his first time in the driver's seat. *Be calm, just go slow, pay attention,* Miles thought, as if he were coaching a sixteen-year-old. *Stay between the lines, tap the brake, coast into the stops…*

Still, he couldn't stop thinking about Aunt Carmen's funeral parlor tongue lashing. *She criticizes me for being angry, but then tells me I'm right. I know the truth! What the hell does Carmen know?*

His eyes nervously scanned the road. Left, right. Left, right. Miles shook his head. *Think of something else…anything else…*He approached a stop sign and conscientiously, gently applied the brake. The car rolled slowly to a halt. The air hung heavy and warm. Miles felt drowsy, his eyelids heavy. He turned down the heat and cracked open the window. A few rogue snowflakes blew in and melted on his cheeks. Miles loosened his tie, unlocked his seatbelt – careful to keep his foot firmly on the brake – and unbuttoned his wool overcoat. He thought fleetingly of taking it off, but remembered the part in "Planes, Trains and Automobiles" with John Candy battling to remove his coat in the car and accidentally setting the car on fire. He cracked a crooked smile as the scene played on his mental movie screen.

But the reprieve didn't last long.

Easy, easy…As he accelerated past the stop sign and back into the light traffic, Aunt Carmen's sharp criticism returned, dragging one of Catherine's stories with it. He'd heard his mother's catalogue of complaints *ad nauseam* growing up – a swirling sea of examples of his mother's emotional crippling. He could recite them verbatim, and often did to Maya. Yet this one was especially significant tonight: how Catherine had been abandoned by the very people she would have expected and had hoped would support her – Aunt Carmen and the other Ayala women.

He took his right hand off the wheel just long enough to flip on the wipers. The snow fell faster. Miles relocked his hands and the words rolled around his head…

Miles reddened with anger remembering how Catherine always wove in tidbits about her childhood, even (especially) to people who had only known her as an adult. Miles suspected she did this on purpose to build her case. To ratchet up the drama. To prove – if only to herself – that her childhood was harder, more difficult, worse than anyone else's.

Your father and I had been fighting again, I don't even remember what about. I couldn't take anymore. I threw a glass at him and ran over to Carmen's house. She only lived three doors down and she was just married too, so we had kind of hit it off at first. All the Ayalas lived in the same two blocks. I always laughed when your dad told me he lived on "Taco Hill" before we started dating, but he wasn't kidding. I knocked. They were all there. Carmen, Aunt Hilda, your cousin Diana. They were always there, not that they ever invited me to come down. They always said it was because they were afraid Michael would get mad, but I knew the truth. They just didn't want me there. Anyway, they were all laughing, talking, dancing back in the kitchen to some rock song on the radio. I don't know what it was. You know I can't stand that garbage. And of course, something delicious was cooking and I hadn't eaten yet, so I was starving. I will never forget how great that house always smelled! I had been crying. My mascara was running down my face. Carmen asked me if I was OK as soon as she saw me. I told her 'No' and went in. I just wanted a friendly ear, a friendly shoulder. Just, a friend.

I told them how bad my life had been, and how bad your dad treated me. But I don't know why I thought they would care about me anymore than anyone else had in my lousy life.

I was only eleven when my mother left me, just when I needed her most. I had just become a woman even though I was very young for that to happen…

(Here, she'd explain that she meant that her period had started, causing yet another cringe-worthy moment for her sons who knew exactly what she meant, but didn't need or want a detailed explanation from their mother.)

When I was in school, we didn't learn about any of that sex stuff like you kids do now! I was terrified and thought I was going to die! I had no idea what was happening to me, if I was sick or hurt. But do you think my mother talked to me about anything, or that I could talk to her? Hell no!

Even now, simply remembering the story alone in the car, Miles cringed at the thought of Catherine's melodramatic mannerisms – how, she would toss her head back, sticking her nose in the air as if someone had just broken wind. As if the story wasn't overblown enough, she also had to overact each part for emphasis. Her affectations were even more irritating because he knew that his maternal grandmother had not actually left Catherine at all. She had just remarried and as often happens, gave most of her time and attention to her new husband. Catherine always made a point to absolve her stepfather for any wrongdoing with her life.

I never had anything against my stepfather. He was a good grandpa to you boys. He never did anything mean to me. He wasn't bad in any way, just in love with your grandmother and demanded her attention like any new husband would. But I needed my mom more than ever. I needed her with me, and she was always someplace else. I mean, not physically, but emotionally. But instead of being able to just be who I was – a normal, eleven-year-old girl – I became the built-in babysitter for my five brothers and sisters. I got tired of that pretty quick. So, I decided to move in with my dad and his new wife. No one really seemed to care either way. I thought the grass would be greener at my father's house. I thought maybe, as his oldest child and daughter, I might have a special place in his heart. I thought I might be his princess. Ha! My mother ignored me, but at least I always knew she still loved me. And if nothing else, I at least held some rank as the eldest child. But my stepmother hated me. I was nothing more than an outsider to her. An intruder stealing her husband's time and attention. She ignored me most of the time, and when she did pay any attention, she was cruel. She'd refuse to get me any new clothes and give me her filthy hand-me-downs which didn't fit me because she was taller than me. And to throw salt on the wound, by the time I moved in, they'd had three kids, so I became the built-in babysitter there, too! First, she took my dad from me, then she took what little freedom and confidence and self-esteem I had. She might have hated me, but I despised her.

I hated my stepmother, but what I hated even more, was us constantly moving to a new town whenever my dad would lose his job — which happened a lot. We'd move supposedly so we could get a fresh start. But let me tell you, nothing ever changed for them, or for me. Unless you consider things getting worse as "changing."

Every place we lived, I never fit in. I was too "City" in one place, then I was too "Country" in another. Which never made any sense to me, because no matter where we went, we were dirt poor. No one ever even tried to be my friend. I was just different. I liked fancy things, and nice clothes. I hated popular music. I loved jazz! Frank Sinatra, Tony Bennett, Ella Fitzgerald, Miles Davis, Charlie Parker, Benny Goodman, they were my favorites.

School was no better. I didn't get very good grades. I didn't care about all that book stuff, but I was smart. I liked to read about all kinds of things besides sports or farming. I paid attention to what was happening in the world. Sometimes when I could get away or pretend that I had to stay after school, I'd sneak down to the library and just sit there, surrounded by all the books. One time, I just opened the dictionary and started with the letter "A" and tried to learn as many new words as I could. But no one cared about me. No one thought about who I was much less who I wanted to be. All I had was my chores at home, watching my rotten brothers and sisters. I dreamed every night about getting out of that house as fast as I could.

Snow and gusty wind pummeled the car. Miles realized with a split second of confusion that he'd somehow misplaced the last few seconds. *Pay attention, goddammit! You can't afford another accident!* A few more minutes passed before another thought surfaced: his mother had been a beautiful young girl made to feel very ugly and old. Suddenly, a spasm squeezed his guts. What was it? Sadness? Guilt? Indigestion? He pulled harder on the wheel and kept driving. His head returned to Catherine's story right where she left it.

I got married the first time when I was eighteen. Not for love, or at least not what you kids today call love. And sure as hell not for money. I would have married just about anyone to get out of that house and away from my stepmother. Your biological father gave me exactly three good things – you, Parker, and an escape from my stepmother.

What could I say? He wasn't much to look at, he had no money to speak of. But getting out of that house meant everything to me. Away from those small-town assholes. He wasn't what you'd call a looker, but he was handsome in a rugged, simple, hard-working, young "Johnny Cash" kind of a way. He was confident. Strong. He carried himself well most of the time. But it didn't take long for my first marriage to go to hell.

I got what I wanted, he got what he wanted. You were born 11 months later – but we were married. Girls didn't get pregnant before marriage then like they do now.

Absolutely not true, Miles knew. Still, he still chuckled at the haughty lengths to which she went to maintain her "pre-marital virginity" even thirty years later, like it mattered.

You were born seventeen days before I turned nineteen. Parker came 16 months later. You looked like your father and Parker looked like me. But it didn't matter who looked like who, Willie wanted nothing to do with any of us. We fought constantly. I was trapped at home watching kids again. The only difference was this time, they were my kids. Willie was too busy doing drugs and drinking and breaking the law to work, so I started working nights as a waitress to support us. A neighbor watched you boys at night, and I watched her kids during the day. Babysitting was what I did best, right?

Miles knew the next part by heart because it still terrified him. Eight months later, Willie kicked in the door to their apartment in a drunken fury, a switchblade in hand.

Then Michael walked in, this young, dark-skinned cop, like a cowboy wearing a white hat. Every night, he'd stop by the restaurant and have a cup of coffee, talk to the manager, check out the customers to make sure everyone was 'safe,' and flirt with all the waitresses. We all knew what he was up to, but it wasn't serious. Until he stopped talking to anyone else and would only sit in my section.

The twinkling, clanging safety arm swung down. *Jesus Christ, a train! On a night like this, that's all I need!* Miles again deliberately eased the car to a stop. It was a slow-moving freight train. He shifted into park, laid back on the head rest, closed his eyes and took a deep breath. The nausea from his bar adventure danced its spiky-heeled encore in his stomach. His mother always flashed a shy, coy smile telling the next part of her story. She was proud that she snagged Michael in the first place. Vanity still had a home in Catherine's soul.

Michael had many bad qualities, but he was handsome. Any woman would have wanted him, and lots did. Including some of the other waitresses. I wasn't trying very hard to get his attention, but I knew he was looking at me, and that made me feel good. Pretty. Like a real woman instead of just a single mother with a criminal for a husband.

Miles felt a little odd thinking of his mother as a "woman," yet as a man, he always secretly understood Michael's interest. Miles had seen pictures of his mother as a young woman. He had to admit, a young Catherine certainly could have attracted any heterosexual male: chestnut hair, high cheekbones, porcelain skin, and a petite hourglass figure. Plus, she had a crystalline, strong, joyful, bluesy, bright singing voice. Bright, yet shadowed with a twinge of sadness. Growing up, he'd hear his mom in the basement singing some jazz or blues tune as she did laundry. Miles remembered being both amazed and vaguely irritated that she did nothing with such immense natural talent.

It didn't take long for your dad to ask me to meet him for breakfast after my shift. But I said no. Many times. I didn't think it was right. I was still married. And I am Catholic. I know religion and vows don't mean much to your generation, but it mattered to me.

That's not to say I wasn't interested, though. Michael was twenty-three, only a couple years older than me, but he already seemed so much, oh, I don't know, more settled. Certain in himself. He bragged about being in the Navy and going to Vietnam, but he was even prouder that he'd come home and become a sheriff's deputy. His older brother, your Uncle Hector, was also a police officer. Michael idolized Hector. Your dad had a lot of good things about him, and my life needed something good. But I kept telling him my life was just too complicated. It wouldn't be fair to him. But he was relentless. He didn't care about my husband or me being divorced, but he immediately cared about you boys.

I believed him when he told me he loved me, but I knew what he really loved was you and your brother. He wanted to be a father.

He would talk about the four of us doing things together, like we were already a family. He wanted me, he wanted you and Parker...but I still said no.

He told me he could make everything simpler if I would just let him. He seemed sincere enough. After a few months of this he finally wore me down. Frankly, by that time, I was so tired of men hitting on me. On those rare occasions when I'd respond at all, the second I mentioned you and your brother waiting for me at home with the babysitter, they'd disappear real fast, which told me all I needed to know about what they really wanted. But not Michael...

I was falling in love. Now, in hindsight, I know it was too easy. I wanted it so bad. For me, for you and your brother. And for him, too. Marrying Michael was the easiest way for all of us to get what we wanted and needed. Boy was I wrong – again!

The train caboose cleared the crossing after fifteen minutes – but what felt like an hour. *Finally!* The red, flashing safety light rose as if to bid a good night to the cars passing under its arm. Miles proceeded cautiously through the intersection. Warming up again, he turned the heat down a few degrees as his mind approached the main part of Catherine's story: the Ayala Women's so-called "betrayal."

I tried to share what was happening to me with Carmen and the girls, so we could bond, become friends, but they already knew – that had to know! They just lived right down the street. Your dad and I fought so much right after we got married. I did everything wrong. And the thing he hated the most was my independence. Oh, he told me a million times how much he admired that in me when he was trying to get me to sleep with him. But now that I was his wife, he just wanted a slave. And whenever I pushed back, he hit back.

I told them this many times. Every, last detail. I was so ashamed! But I just wanted someone – anyone – to take my side and say that they understood about your dad, what I was going through. I should have known better than to think that any of those Ayala women would care. Back then, I was the only white woman in the family. Of course, later, when three or four of the wives were white, then it wasn't such a big deal anymore. No one criticized them for not speaking Spanish, or not cooking Mexican food, or taking care of their Mexican man like he was used to. Oh no! But I was the first, so I got all the nasty comments and filthy looks! I did everything those girls asked for. Diana used to smoke but Rodrigo didn't like it. So, she'd sneak down to our house and tell him that I needed her to watch one of you boys, so she could have a cigarette. But did I ever say anything? No!

Those girls weren't all sweet little angels either. I can't tell you how many times one of them would go to a party or a bar – sometimes even with another man – and I never said a word! I understood. They just wanted to live a little and have something in their lives besides just being some man's wife and slave. But when I wanted the same thing, you know who stood up for me? No one. They all just told me to ignore it or get used to it. All of it. Including when your father would hit me or call me terrible names because I wanted to get a part-time job just to get out of the house a little bit. We couldn't even have friends over because he didn't trust me around any other man. I didn't know which way to turn. I had no one then, and I have no one now. And I will never forgive them. Never!

Having worked herself into a blizzard of self-pity and denial, Catherine would routinely cap her story with the greatest sin of all: blaming him and Parker for marrying Michael and holding them responsible for the heartache and pain that followed.

I could have married anyone I wanted to. Someone who loved me for me! There were lots of men who promised me anything I wanted. A big house! Money! An easy life! One even promised to make me a big music star. I could have had someone who would have made me happy. But I married your father for you and Parker!

Miles remembered this rant as clearly as if Catherine were sitting next to him in the car. She made the claim so often it became a venomous mantra. The words ripped at Miles' heart, fueling a flaming anger toward his mother doused only by deflating guilt. His mind again asked the question it had asked a million times. The question that he, in late adolescence even once screwed up the courage to fling directly at her. *How can you possibly blame us? I was just a toddler. Parker was a baby! Jesus Christ, even if we begged you to marry Dad, you could have married a million other guys and we would never have known the difference! We were just kids! You were the adult!*

Miles pulled the car to the side of the road again. He slammed the gear shift into "Park" and pushed the button to turn on the Emergency flashers. The realization that he'd missed the cold truth behind Catherine's laments for all those years now hit him in the face like an icy, gravel-filled snowball. His heartbeat like he'd just run a marathon. The car's interior swam around his eyes and he couldn't catch a full breath. He put his hands back on the wheel and lowered his head until he felt the cool leather just above his eyebrows.

Miles knew his mother's modus operandi. Could anticipate her emotional, finger-pointing tendencies.

Catherine's stories were undeniably overblown, melodramatic, accusatory. Yet, tonight, Miles slowly came to understand something he'd never even considered before:

They were also too heartbreaking to be fake.

Humiliation, confusion and anger consumed him like lightening striking a dry, late-summer field. *What have I done? I'm such a horrible person. I'm the oldest son. I'm supposed to protect my mother and I have made everything worse!*

"Goddamn it all to hell!" His exploding voice fractured the bleak silence and shocked even him.

Several cars edged gingerly past. None offered help, though that was fine. Miles couldn't have talked to anyone through the choking gag of his failing.

Miles pointedly avoided using the word "hate."

Only four letters, yet big enough to crush souls and civilizations, "hate" was, like many clichés, overused. However, he openly admitted hating one thing:

The lifetime of guilt Catherine had hung around his neck.

Tonight, he would consider adding another:

The possibility that he'd been wrong about his mother.

Nearing his house, Miles stared out the window, confused by his surroundings. For a few jumbled seconds he experienced the opposite of déjà vu. Nothing was familiar. As if he'd never driven down these streets or seen these houses, front yards, trees. He shook his head, unnerved but relieved to be home safe…eased into his driveway…turned off the lights and the engine…laid his head back…closed his eyes…waited for the mental fog to blow away. Finally, time and place and context fell back in line. His breathing calmed. He stepped out of the car and trudged to his back porch, amazed that three or so inches of snow had fallen during his ride home.

He inched up the steps, not terribly anxious to find out if Maya had beaten him home. A light burned inside the kitchen window. Miles couldn't remember now if they had left it on when they left for the wake. He tentatively inserted the key into the deadbolt and grabbed the doorknob, but before he could turn it, Maya filled the doorway and blocked his entry like a brick wall.

"Hi, honey," Miles squeaked, evoking an apologetic tone.

Maya did not suffer fools, not even on her best days. This day had been lightyears away from one of her best.

"Don't say another word to me, Miles Ayala!" she hissed into the snowy winter darkness.

"Listen, I am so sorry." He tried to take her hand. "I know I was wrong for…"

Maya yanked her hand back like she'd touched a live wire. She locked her arms across her chest.

"Oh really? You know you're wrong? What was your first clue? The seventeen shades of embarrassment on my face? Your mother sobbing in the other room? Or" – she unfolded one arm and jabbed a sharp-nailed index finger into his chest – "the stains on your clothes from the food fight you had with Benjie, in public. You're sorry alright. You're a sorry excuse for a man, and a husband, and a son. You should be ashamed of yourself!"

"I know, I really…"

"Shut up! I told you, I don't want to hear anything from you. I have been listening to you complain and whine and mope for a week! I love you with all my heart, but you have been a complete asshole to *everyone*, and *everyone* is sick of it. Your family, your friends and half the bar you threw up in last night!"

She shifted in the doorway so that the kitchen light created a corona around her. Miles thought she looked like the sun about to explode.

"I only have one question, and if you answer wrong, you can just get back in your car and find a hotel."

He dropped his head and didn't dare look up.

"Yes. One question. I understand," he mumbled, his reply nearly lost against the shushing of the swirling snow, falling even heavier.

She firmly cupped and lifted Miles' chin and locked eyes with him.

"Fine. Here it is. It's very simple, so don't screw it up: You have been acting like a child for days," Maya said. "Are you finally ready to act like a man?"

<u>17</u>

The snow that clung to his overcoat seconds ago now filled puddles on their kitchen floor.

Maya closed the kitchen door behind Miles and brushed past him without a word.

"Thank you." Miles cautiously reached out to Maya.

"For what?" she said, backing up a step.

"Well, for letting me in, for starters."

"That's stupid. I wasn't going to let you freeze outside."

"I know, but still, just, thank you. I…"

Maya glared at her husband.

"Miles, I am in absolutely no mood. It's late and we have a long day tomorrow. We have to help bury your father in the morning, in case you'd forgotten."

"I know, I know. I just wanted to say how much I love you."

No response.

"And that I appreciate everything you've done for

me this week."

Nothing.

"I don't know what I'd do without you."

Maya shifted from one heel to the other, a wordless stare her only reply. Finally, she turned and started toward their bedroom.

"I am truly sorry. I am such an idiot sometimes!"

Maya didn't break stride. "I know."

"You know? Which part?"

"Both" She started to climb the stairs. "And don't wake me when you come up."

Sighing, Miles kicked off his shoes and slung his wet coat over the back of a kitchen chair near the heating vent. The clock on the face of the stove blinked:

2 a.m.

He started heating water for a cup of black tea, hoping it would power him through what promised to be a long night of work. Waiting for the water to boil, he considered his most recent marital faux pas – and his wife's tough love. She was truly a kind and sweet-hearted woman, and Miles wanted no life that did not include her. She always forgave in the end, but Miles knew from experience that Maya Ayala rarely forgot. An expert tactician on the marital battlefield, she held moments like these and wielded them as weapons hours, days, weeks, even years later in new battles he couldn't even imagine now, much less anticipate.

Finally, the teapot burbled. Miles poured the steaming water over the teabag and headed to his office. He settled into his chair, turned on the computer and sighed. "Ok, here we go…"

Miles covered his mouth to stifle an involuntary laugh – he did not want to wake the dragon.

The page on the computer screen, blank and empty as his head, waited to be filled.

"But really," he whispered into the dusky room. "How hard can it be? I've written thousands of things. Stories, plays, speeches, scripts. This is just one more."

This is supposed to be a celebration of his father. A way to put him on a pedestal and keep him there for his mom's sake. But Miles struggled for the words. What could he say now about his father in death, when he had so little good to say about him in life?

Where to start, where to start? What's going to really grab them?

Unsure, he tried dropping a few nuggets about Michael's childhood:

"We didn't know a lot about him, but what we knew, was awesome. Dad was a first generation Mexican American. He grew up on the poor side of Jordan. He was beloved – and spoiled beyond measure – as the baby of the family. My dad was the only child of a single mother in the 1940s when single parenting was still a shameful secret. She died when she was very young, so, his grandparents raised him as their own. Aunts and uncles became siblings, cousins became aunts and uncles…You have never seen such a twisted family tree! Still, he was extremely proud of who he was and where he came from. So much so, that he never left. He served in the military just as several of his uncles and male cousins had. His older brother Hector was the first Mexican cop on the Jordan Police Department. Dad was so proud that he followed his brother into a law enforcement career himself."

Too dry…sounds like an encyclopedia entry… Miles rubbed his scruffy, unshaven face. *Need something more human…more dramatic…*

Then it came to him in a flash.

His fingers flicked at the keyboard, hesitantly at first, then faster as thoughts and ideas filled his head.

"Parker and I do not resemble our father in the least. Yet, I always knew he was our dad and that he loved us because he told us in the most profound way possible: by marrying our mom and giving us his name."

Yea, that's good. Tight, clean, powerful.

"I look nothing like my last name. I know this because many people have told me that as they stared at my brown eyes and hair, my white skin – although I do get a decent tan in the summer. The secret was undeniably out when they tried to speak Spanish to me and got nothing in return. Benjie is the only one of us with even one of our dad's actual genes, but more times than I knew people would say how Parker and I looked just like dad. I used to think, 'Two white kids, a Mexican man…were these people blind? Stupid? Being nice? Or had we somehow started to look like our dad, absorbing some aspect of his appearance, like pets and their owners?'"

Miles' fingers danced over the keyboard. Soon he typed so fast and hard he was afraid the clicking and clacking might wake Maya and earn him another reprimand. But his hands seemed to have taken a life of their own.

"No one ever talked about us being adopted. Once it was done, it was as if it had never happened. We were immediately and unquestioningly accepted – two white branches grafted onto a Mexican family tree. Dad would go to ridiculous lengths to paint himself as our biological father, telling elaborate and often hilarious tall tales about how we were born as if he had really been there. And I guess, in a way, he had been. He told these crazy tall tales not to cover up a scandal. Exactly the opposite. He told them because he was immensely proud of his new family, and wanted everyone to know that these boys were, indeed, his, by every measure. I like to say that I am Mexican more by background than by blood. Yet, I am extremely proud to be an Ayala, even if it's only on paper and in spirit."

Miles pushed back from the desk and stared at the words. He cracked his knuckles. An evening's dose of tension escaped noisily from his suddenly-aching, tight fingers.

He smiled. "That's good stuff. Really, really good stuff."

Then, doubt rolled in like early morning fog.

Suddenly, surprisingly, something didn't feel quite right. He re-read a few sentences through blurring eyes… Had he left something out? Put too much in? Told the wrong stories? Confused details? After all, a lot of what he thought he knew about his dad was often little more than family lore. Sure, he loved and respected his dad, appreciated what Michael had done for him and Parker. Yet the truth was, they'd only really bonded in the last couple of years – over Miles' children, Michael's first grandchildren. That made sense in a way that at first brought Miles a measure of quiet, prideful joy, but now seemed somehow thin and a bit sad.

He scrolled back to the top of the page, slowly turning each word in his mind. Making sure each said exactly what he wanted to say, exactly as he wanted to say it.

Still, he couldn't escape the nagging truth – the same truth he'd battled all week in his heart and head. Heck, most of his life. That his father had dark sides that no one else, save him and his mother seemed to ever see. Miles felt like he was sliding backwards down a hill, shoved by Temptation to shine a light on his father's sharp edges. To tell the inconvenient – even bitter – truth. Finally, he slapped himself across the cheek. *No! I promised Aunt Carmen that I'd do the right thing for Mom!*

In a cloudy corner of his mind, Miles thought he heard a faint ringing. He kept writing. The sound persisted. Miles raised his eyes from the screen, turned his head and caught his desk clock out of the corner of his eye:

5 a.m.

Then he remembered: Maya was in bed.

"Oh crap!"

He jumped from his chair, raced through the family room and lunged at the phone on the end table next to the couch.

"*Hello!*" he answered in a hoarse whisper, making no effort to hide his irritation. "Mom? Do you know what time it is?"

<u>18</u>

Words, words, words…so many words…

A large audience of Ayala family and friends, coworkers from Michael's three-decade long law enforcement career and faces Miles did not recognize – *Probably criminal informants* – sat in neat rows at the front of the funeral home chapel. Flowers lined the walls nearly to ceiling, all sent in his dad's memory, conveying well wishes, praying for comfort. But it wasn't the flowers that commanded his attention, it was the hundreds of eyes staring at him, waiting for words about his dad.

Now, after a week of consternation, Miles had those words. They'd flooded his head after Maya had reluctantly let him back into their house. Three hours of work had produced about two thousand words of finely crafted wisdom, humor and comfort. He stood ready to deliver the eulogy that his mother requested – begged for; demanded – with all the practiced eloquence, grace and charm he'd learned as a professional public speaker.

He inhaled...opened his mouth...but could not raise his head. The words, dense with the dark matter of a lifetime of confusion, criticism, anxiety and anger, held his eyes like the gravity from a collapsing star. He stared blankly at the notecards, riffling through them, searching for something, but unsure what that something was. *What the hell? I've spoken to groups a million times and suddenly now I can't speak?*

Then, as if God had had enough of this nonsense, the cards exploded from Miles' hands. Some fell on the podium. Three fluttered onto Michael's casket, parked between Miles and the mourners. Most landed on the floor.

"Oh shit!"

A few gasps and what he immediately recognized as a belly laugh from Parker peppered the titters from the crowd.

"Er...I mean...Um..." Miles spluttered. Maya glared at him with wide-eyed exasperation. Catherine bore her standard scowl. He reached over the podium, retrieved the notecards nesting on the casket, then picked up the cards from the floor. Standing back up, he cracked his head on the podium's sharp edge.

"Goddamn it!" he yelped.

A good second passed before he realized what he'd said. He grabbed the back of his head and felt something warm oozing in his hair. The mild titters of a second ago quickly became full-throated chuckles. Miles shook his head to clear away the fog and sharp pain. At another time, in another context, happening to someone else, this would have been a moment of pure hilarity, but right now, happening to him, it wasn't funny. Not at all. He waited for the room to settle, took a deep breath, and started.

"Good morning." Just speaking brought a grimace thanks to the growing throb at the back of his neck.

"My name is Miles Ayala. As Michael's oldest son, I want to thank everyone for coming this morning on behalf of my mother, Catherine, my brothers Parker and Benjie, and our whole family." He looked again at Maya. What he found on her face wasn't exactly forgiveness but was a vast improvement from last night's frozen fury. *Thank you, thank you, thank you. I love you more than you will ever know…*

"I also want to apologize for the, um, slight disturbance I caused yesterday."

"Ha," Benjie sneered, low but loud enough for Miles to hear.

Staring daggers at his youngest brother, Miles continued. "My mom asked me to share a few thoughts about my dad." He looked down at his cards for a quick reminder. His eyes settled on the casket as he drew another deep, time-killing breath.

"Many of you know – I mean, knew – my dad as a police officer, neighbor, relative and friend. I am sure we all agree that Michael Ayala was a great man, husband and father. But no matter how we knew him…"

Miles stopped. He stared again at the notecards he held as if he'd never seen them before. As if he'd never seen written words of any language. He stared hard at Maya, silently begging for telepathic help as if he'd had a stroke right there at the podium.

Then, more words – familiar from a week of repetition, but now unexpected, unplanned, unwelcome – flared in his mind. *I can't do this...I can't do this...*

"I...I'm..."

Miles cleared his throat, now dry as Arizona in August.

"I'm sorry. I can't do this."

"What? Oh, for crying out loud! Here we go again!" Benjie said, his disgust clear over the rumbling confusion.

"No!" Miles nearly shouted. "That's not what I mean." He reviewed his notecards again, but they may as well have been blank. He abandoned his speech altogether and quickly tucked the cards into the inside pocket of his jacket.

"I just mean, you all might think you knew my dad, but you didn't know the real Michael Ayala, and neither did I. And I can't stand up here and say that my dad was this angelic figure because it wasn't true."

He grasped the podium's edges to steady himself and leaned toward the microphone.

"Let me correct myself. It is true, or at least, mostly true. Yes, he was a good cop – no, check that: he was a great cop. Yes, he was a good dad. And yes, he could even be a decent husband sometimes." He glanced at Catherine in the front row. Her face, so often carved by anger, softened. She lowered her eyes, perhaps unable to look directly at this fact after denying it for so long.

"Michael Ayala was one giant, walking Mexican contradiction. He could be an incredibly kind, thoughtful and generous person. But he was also a hard, mean, even cruel person with an abusive, unpredictable temper. He treated many people very badly – including a lot of you here in this room today. But he had an incredible sense of humor. Man, he could leave you gasping for breath from laughter. Still, what he thought was funny was often very hurtful, even cruel." Miles noticed a few quick nods of recognition. He gazed sharply now on Parker, who never deigned nor dared to admit Michael's shortcomings. Miles knew it was too much work – and too painful – for Parker to bring their dad down from his pedestal.

"Just look how he was with normal people. If he liked you, it didn't matter if you were Charles Manson, my dad liked you forever. More times than I care to remember people came to our door who should have been, and probably just were in jail – felons, convicts, gangbangers, drug dealers. I don't mind telling you it was a little scary. But he welcomed them, invited them into our house, asked them to eat with us, talked to them like they were old friends."

A few chuckles floated from the seats. "You think I'm kidding, but I'm not. Right, mom?" Catherine finally looked at Miles and allowed the slightest shade of a smile.

"But if my dad didn't like you, forget about it. You could be Jesus Christ himself and he wouldn't let you on the porch much less in the house to break bread – literally or figuratively." More laughter. Miles smiled at his own unintended pun. He suddenly felt lighter than he had in a week. Like he'd lost fifty psychic pounds. He stepped away from the podium, his spirit untethered.

Freed by the confidence that came only through truth. Not anger. Not vengeance. Not reproach. But simple, clear, irrefutable honesty.

"He was like that with everything. He came from a family of Mexican immigrants but could be the biggest racist I ever knew. He dedicated his life to protecting people's rights but violated people's rights lots of times. And I don't just mean our rights as teens!" That one got a smile from both his brothers. Miles returned their grins.

"He insisted how his family came before everything but would leave us at the drop of a hat – sometimes in the middle of dinner or a family event – to go help someone out or worse, meet with some informant. He'd preach about the importance of church, but I swear to you I can count on one hand the number of times he actually *went* to church – and three of those were my wedding and the baptisms of my two kids."

More laughter as mourners recognized the Michael Ayala that Miles knew only too well. He waited for calm, then spoke again, his voice barely above a whisper.

"The fact of the matter is, Michael Ayala wasn't a saint by any measure. Not like a lot of you people want to think and need to believe." He again eyed Parker in his seat.

"But he wasn't a devil either. You know who reminded me of that? The person who has the least reason to. The person he was often the meanest to, the one he treated worse than just about anyone short of the criminals he arrested. Our mom."

Miles couldn't look at Catherine now, but he knew

she was listening intently. He quickly debated how deeply to delve into this mine, but decided that, in this case, less was more. She'd suffered enough. Endured enough.

"Suffice it to say, their relationship was often rocky. Which is not to say that my dad was totally responsible for their marital difficulties. Anyone who knows my mother knows that she is, well, shall we say," – Miles dramatically raised his eyes to the ceiling and cupped his chin in his right hand, as if searching for just the right phrase – "*complex.*" Many of the mourners howled. Having known Catherine for years. They got the joke. They'd lived it.

"She called me at five this morning to make sure I was alright and see how I was doing on this eulogy. I told her I'd been working on it all night. It was fine. Well-written, funny, sad, blah-blah-blah, but I still wasn't totally happy with it. You know what she said? 'Then don't do it.' I nearly dropped the phone! I would have screamed if Maya wasn't sleeping. But before I could remind her that she'd been hounding me for a week to do this, she told me a story about my dad. Something I hadn't thought about in forever."

Miles paused again. "The acorn wars. You guys remember, right?" He grinned and his eyes widened as he peered at his siblings.

He circled away from the podium again and crossed in front of the casket, stopping in front of the first row of mourners. He reached out to Catherine, took her hand and held it for a few gentle seconds.

"See, when we were growing up there was a giant oak

tree in our front yard. Come fall, that sucker would drop thousands and thousands of acorns everywhere. One of our chores was to clean all those acorns. We had buckets and buckets of acorns. So many, we didn't know what to do with them." Miles now swept from one end of the front row to the other like a rock star playing the crowd. His eyes glittered with the memory. *Now this is more like it! They're eating up every word!*

"One of us, I'm not sure who, got the bright idea to hide those buckets in the garage, around the outside of the house, in the bushes – and to attack Dad when he came home from work. Man, we hid behind cars and trees and around corners. Parker even got up on the garage roof. We bombed Dad like there was no tomorrow! He ran away like a sissy with his tail between his legs, yelling for Mom to save him. We knew we had won – until the next day, when Dad came home. We carpet bombed him again. He ran in the house again, crying and screaming like a baby. And just as we stopped laughing and caught our breath, he barrel-assed out the back door, both hands filled with acorns." Miles doubled over, slapping his leg in time with his own laughter. He pointed to his brothers. "Remember that guys?" They nodded.

"Sometime after we went to bed, he had snuck outside, found one of our buckets and hid it in the basement for the next day. We learned all about the element of surprise that day. This went on for several days until he made the mistake of chasing us through the house one day throwing acorns everywhere. I can still see it: a twisting line of Parker, me, Benjie and Dad, followed by Mom yelling at us to get out of her house, like something out of a Keystone Cops or Charlie Chaplin movie."

Miles basked in the eruption of laughter.

"Anyway, this became something of a tradition. No one knew exactly when, or what would trigger it – but every year when those acorns started to fall, we kept an extra sharp eye on our dad, because we knew what was coming – and that we couldn't trust him as far as we could see him. If he ever left the room, we knew he was up to something."

Miles turned, gently laid his hands on the casket, and took a long moment to collect himself. Soberly now, he continued.

"Look, I am going to be very honest. This has been a very hard week for me, and not only because my dad died. He was a mystery to me, in the same way, I guess that all parents are mysteries to their children. The truth is, in a lot of ways, I don't know who my father is – or was. Knowing that Parker and I were adopted adds even more distance between us. At least it does for me. Because of that I sometimes felt – feel – like I don't know who I am either. I know this doesn't make sense to a lot of you, especially to my brothers. In some ways it doesn't make sense to me either, and I have spent a lot of time and energy trying to sort all this out. I may have even bothered a few of you in the process of doing that."

"You think so?" Parker snorted.

"Say it," Benjie half laughed, half yelled. "You were a jackass!"

"And I apologize for that, too." In the end, Miles

knew he could always count on his brothers for moral and comedic support, even if it came as his own expense.

He let the room settle, then looked right to left, from his mother, to his wife, to both of his brothers, before settling on his Aunt Carmen.

"A very wise woman who I love dearly told me yesterday that my mom and dad are both heroes for what they did and sacrificed and accepted to create a family. *Our* family." Another pause.

"I don't know about 'heroes.' But I know this: Michael Ayala did a lot of questionable things as a husband. No one can deny that. Still, he did a lot of great things as a father. Including fighting those 'ridiculous acorn wars' with his boys, as my mom reminded me this morning. He knew the value of making time to just be silly with his children, no matter how long his day had been or whatever else was happening. It was the most important thing to us, so it became the most important thing to him. I still have a lot of questions about our relationship and who I am as a man, husband and son. But I can tell you without a doubt that I would be very proud to be the kind of father who makes time to throw a few million acorns with his kids."

Miles glanced again at Catherine. Her makeup – almost always flawless – showed the slightest trail of a tear down her cheek. This time, she did not turn away.

<u>19</u>

"Come on, honey," Maya said. "People are starting to arrive."

She cupped Miles' elbow trying to gently guide him back from the gaping grave. They'd arrived at the cemetery a few minutes ahead of the rest of the procession which, led by dozens of law enforcement vehicles had driven by Michael and Catherine's house in a final farewell.

Car doors opened and closed behind them. Somber small talk formed steam clouds that quickly evaporated into the bitter mid-January chill.

"I know, it's just…"

He looked in the grave again. The hole appeared bottomless.

The flag-draped casket seemed to float above the hole, resting on the steel rigging cleverly disguised as fake grass. His mother (actually, Michael's insurance, which wasn't bad considering his career as a mid-level local government employee) had bought a better-than-average burial package – appearances remained vitally important to her, even (especially) at the end of Michael's life.

Still, it looked like any other casket he'd ever seen. Except that it wasn't. How could it possibly be? This one held what remained of his father. Their life together. Whatever had linked them. Conversations and debates and arguments and jokes and laughter and advice and congratulations and condolences and smiles and tears shared, and not ever now to be shared again.

Yet, this casket was the same as countless others. It, too, would soon be swallowed by the earth, succumbing to the irrefutable truth of Time: man, made arrogant by the false gods of money and power and medicine and technology, may win life's battles.

But Death always wins the war.

Miles turned to his wife. His eyes crinkled against the painfully sharp blue sky. He stared at her face – the deep eyes, slightly-pouty lips and cold-pinked cheeks. He turned again toward the grave.

"What's wrong? Did you lose your keys? What's down there?" she chirped, trying to lighten the moment.

"Very funny." He grinned to signal that he appreciated her kindness. Yet Miles didn't know what to say that wouldn't sound stupid, or worse. *Yes, I'm looking for something. I'm looking for answers, but I don't even know the question…*

He turned, put his hands on her waist, now thicker with the heavy winter coat the day required – biting cold, despite the incredible sunshine – and gently kissed the person who had seen and accepted and forgiven more of his knife-edged facets than any other.

"Don't worry about me, I'm fine. I just want this day to be over. I love you more than anything in the world. Thank you again for understanding me last night."

"Please, let's not go there again," Maya ribbed. She kissed him back, slowly, warming his lips. "Your grandmother just got here. Go help her to her chair and sit with her. I know how close you two are."

Indeed, Miles adored his maternal grandmother. Twice married, a survivor of the Great Depression, World War Two and many challenges even worse, Rachel Steele was perhaps his favorite person in the world next to his wife.

"Hi there, beautiful lady!" Miles called to Rachel. He trudged through the snow-covered cemetery lawn. Suddenly he realized that this was the first day since Michael died that it wasn't snowing. The grass, miraculously still green in spots, did its best to peek out where feet had broken through the covering.

She offered her usual reply as he approached. "Why, hello sir!"

"Here, let me help you." Miles guided his grandmother toward the edge of the tent-covered plot where Michael's service would be held.

"Thank you, but you don't have to do that," Rachel said. "I'm not that old – yet."

"And you never will be," Miles said. "But it's my responsibility as your oldest – and favorite – grandchild to help you whenever I can."

He took her right hand and led her carefully across the artificial turf in front of the casket to the front row of seats.

"Now, don't say that. You know I love all of my grandchildren equally," Rachel said.

"I understand." He wrapped his left arm around her back, gave her a gentle squeeze, a sly smile and an exaggerated, conspiratorial wink as if to say, "Your secret is safe with me."

Of course, she'd never explicitly said he was her favorite. How could she, Miles knew, without hurting the feelings of one or another of her twenty-eight grandkids? Still, in his heart he knew the truth. After all, she'd also never explicitly denied it, either.

Holding her hand firmly, he helped his grandmother settle on Catherine's left. Miles sat in the hard, white – and now cold – plastic folding chair between his grandmother on his right and Maya.

Rachel touched her oldest daughter's knee. "Catherine, take off your sunglasses. You don't need them," she ordered. She offered no other greeting or condolence. They certainly loved each other, Miles knew, but their relationship was still, after all these years, often defined by tension and obligatory respect. Mutual affection fell lower on the list.

"I will when things get started," Catherine said. Her gloved left hand dabbed at her eyes and nose with a damp, mascara-splotched tissue.

As Maya, Parker, Benjie and the rest of the immediate Ayala family gathered in the first rows, Miles surveyed the crowd. At least two hundred people clustered under and around the edges of the tented service area. Not as many as yesterday-understandable given the biting temperatures – but still more than he'd ever seen.

"I can't believe how many people came out, with the weather and all," he whispered to Maya.

"Why not? Lots and lots and lots of people loved your dad. I would think you would have realized that by now," she quietly scolded.

The buzz of small talk faded as their parish priest Father John Meadows stepped in front of the casket. Holding a Bible in two gloved hands, he shivered through a greeting.

"Good morning, Catherine, Miles, Parker, Benjamin, and to all of Michael's family, friends, coworkers and associates. We are gathered here today as family in Christ. Family who loved this man, this son, husband, father, friend and public servant. We all mourn the passing of his life to heaven, but we also celebrate the joy and camaraderie and love he gave us in his time here on earth."

The priest removed and handed his gloves to an altar boy. He stepped over to Catherine, stooped and cupped her left hand between his. Startled by the small gesture, she looked up and removed her sunglasses with her other hand, revealing eyes swollen from a lifetime of tears shed in the last few hours.

"As some of you know, I also serve as the police chaplain, so I was blessed to count myself among the many, many people that Michael helped and cared for over the years," the priest said.

He paused and held her gaze for a few seconds.

"Whatever his human failings," he said, talking directly to Catherine, "we must remember Michael was a child of God. As we all are. None of us are perfect, but he truly had a servant's heart which, in my book, puts him head and shoulders above many of us. I think the large turnout here today is testament to the love so many felt for him."

Father Meadows straightened and exhaled a plume of frozen breath. He began reciting the Catholic funeral service, crossing himself, head to chest, shoulder to shoulder. "In the name of the Father, and of the Son, and of the Holy Ghost…"

Miles knew this service nearly by heart, having heard it several times in his adolescence and young adulthood, yet he felt somehow disconnected from everything happening around him. He saw the priest's mouth move and he reflexively repeated the rote gestures. When he wasn't standing or sitting or crossing himself, he held his grandmother's hand as if it were a rope tied to a fur-covered life preserver.

Father Meadows completed the proscribed introductory service elements then finally started his homily. He locked eyes with Miles, forcing him to listen. Meadows pointedly looked at and spoke directly to each family member. *This guy's good…* When the priest moved on to Parker, Miles stole a look through the tent's open back. An evergreen draped in crystalline snow from top to bottom towered over everything around it. Miles couldn't look away from that tree. He tilted toward Maya. "Look at that tree. That thing has got to be forty or fifty feet tall," he whispered.

"What?"

"That tree right in front of us. It's huge. It looks like

something is moving but I don't see anything there."

"I have no idea what you are talking about," Maya growled between gritted teeth. "Please focus and pay attention!" She glared at her husband and jerked her head toward the priest who had circled back to Miles.

"I know it's hard for some people to hear someone try to offer words of comfort in a moment like this. It's even harder to hear a priest talk about things like marriage and parenting. Some would say we lack any authority in such matters, without no real point of reference. That's an occupational hazard, I guess. But one thing I know, because we all know it, is what it means to lose a parent," Meadows said.

This time, he only glanced for a second at Parker and Benjie before his gaze fixed back on Miles.

"When someone dies, you just want to make sense out of it, but you can't. I think of it this way: the human body is a machine. Perhaps the best machine ever made. Usually, it works just the way it was designed. But all machines break. Most of the time, we can take the machine to a mechanic – in this case, a doctor – who can fix it right up, good as new. But at some point, the machine can't be fixed anymore. We call that death. Our heads know this. It's logical. It makes sense. But try explaining logic to our hearts, right?" Meadows smiled at his little joke, drawing a few light, rueful chuckles.

"Now when a parent dies, that's a problem of another magnitude. Not only are we losing a loved one, we're losing a presence that defines and identifies and claims and marks us. Something that made everything right when it was wrong. Something that seemed, in our little sphere, perfect. Now, that's our hearts talking."

The priest closed his Bible and stared for a moment at the tarp covering the frozen ground. "Our very real challenge," he resumed, "is to admit, despite our hubris, that our heads are right. We were made in God's image, but we're not gods. God didn't make us perfect. God made us human. It's a long road between the reality of imperfection and the ideal of perfection. And if we're ever to get there – and I am not saying we ever do, or even can – then we do so through our imperfections."

Miles saw a lot of confused looks and stared back at Father Meadows.

"Now I know this all sounds like the kind of college philosophy gobbledygook you'd normally discuss over a bottle of red wine, but follow me on this because it's important," Meadows said. "Realizing and confessing with sincere humility that we make mistakes makes us work all the harder to be better people. The ability to see ourselves for who we are, and the chance to improve ourselves is a great gift from God. God accepts and forgives us our imperfections. What a wonderful and awesome gift. That is truly God's grace in our lives, given to each of us, every day. I know, accepting such a gift can sometimes be hard. It can be even harder to give that same gift to others. But that's what God wants us to do. Believe it or not, God wants us to re-gift!" Again, the priest laughed at his joke.

"He wants us to forgive others for their sins just as He forgives us for ours. This is essential. For, in forgiveness we create our truest identity, we realize our own freedom. We create the perfection of heaven through our flawed humanity."

Father Meadows re-opened his Bible and stepped back to the center of the front row. "I don't profess to know everything about Michael Ayala, but I know this much. He was a good man, deserving of our love, our respect, our admiration. And most of all, our forgiveness. Amen."

The priest's words hung clear and sharp and true in front of Miles, who sat frozen in silence.

He shook his head and tried to remember what remained of the service. Two United States Marines would soon remove the flag from his dad's casket, fold it into a tight triangle, present it to Catherine and offer their condolences on behalf of a grateful nation for Michael's military service. Everyone would then pile back into their cars and head to the hall for the reception. Finally, the end was near, Miles thought.

Suddenly, the air exploded.

What the hell? Miles realized he'd forgotten about the twenty-one-gun salute given at veterans' funerals. Everyone turned toward the back of the tent. Standing about twenty feet away, seven Marines fired rifles into the air three times in quick succession as a Marine bugler sounded the somber notes of "Taps." Everyone stood. The military veterans and police officers snapped a crisp salute toward the ear-splitting volley.

Then he felt something foreign on his face. Something wet. Had snow blown onto his cheek? Had a bird pooped on him? *Can't be, we're under a tent…* Quickly, the drop built and became a rushing torrent. He cried as if he'd never cried before. Tears gushed in crashing waves down his face and neck and into his coat and scarf. In a flash it occurred to him that he hadn't cried since he'd laid on his father's newly lifeless body at the hospital a week before. Miles turned and collapsed into his grandmother's mink-covered shoulder, struggling to breathe between wrenching sobs.

"Oh, honey!" Rachel gently stroked Miles' hair for several minutes. Wordless, universal comfort for intimate grief that defied words. "Shh, it's alright. Go ahead, let it out," she consoled as if he were six years old and had hurt his knee. Finally, when it seemed like he'd squeezed every drop of water from his body, Miles raised his head, eyes red, cheeks raw and wet and cold.

"Grandma, I'm so sorry! I don't know what happened. One minute everything was fine and then those guns went off. I guess I wasn't expecting that."

Rachel gently cradled his face in her hands, wiping his eyes and nose with a tissue. *Like mother, like daughter,* Miles thought. Then, in a tone both firm and soft, she chided her oldest grandchild. "Miles Ayala, you have been through a lot this week. You have nothing to apologize for."

He stared at his grandmother. Adoration now replaced tears in his eyes. Then he looked at her shoulder. The brown mink where his head had just nestled was now a moist, matted mess. "Oh, my goodness, I am so sorry about your coat," he said, embarrassed.

"Don't you worry about my coat. I'll get it dry cleaned, and I won't even charge you for it," Rachel said, then smiled. "After all, you are my favorite grandchild."

THE ACORN WARS

<u>20</u>

The last few cars meandered along the snowy road toward the cemetery gates. Miles remained in his plastic chair near the gravesite, alternately staring at Michael's still-floating coffin and the mysterious evergreen tree behind it.

"Honey," Maya said. "Are you ready to go? Everyone is headed back to the hall, and I am sure your mother will want to count every piece of chicken they eat."

Miles chuckled. "It's funny," he said, "because it's true." He sighed and stood, then stopped and laid his hand on the now-flagless coffin one more time. "Goodbye, Dad, I hope you know how much I love you."

"He does, sweetie. I know he does."

Maya took her husband's arm and started to march him toward their car.

"Excuse me, sir?"

Miles turned back. A short, middle-aged Hispanic

man called from near the service tent. "Yes?"

Miles felt like he knew the man but could not place him. "I'm sorry, I don't mean to be rude, but you look very familiar. Have we met?"

"No sir, I don't think so," said the man with a slight Mexican accent. "My name is Roberto Marquez. I am the chief groundskeeper. Please accept my condolences for your loss."

"Thank you," Miles said, while thinking, *Enough condolences. I am hungry and tired, and I just want to be done…*

"I'm so sorry to bother you with this today, but I need some final paperwork signed. Mrs. Ayala was already in the car and said she had to get to the reception before the crowd arrived to make sure everything was right," Marquez said.

Miles and Maya looked at each other and smiled.

"She told me to have you sign everything. Is that alright with you?"

"What is it?"

"Just some information about burial procedures, what we will do when the ground thaws in the spring, visitation rules. Stuff like that."

"Well, I guess, if it's alright with you."

"As long as you're part of the immediate family, that's all I need," the groundskeeper said. He handed Miles a clipboard and a pen.

The tree behind the funeral tent suddenly erupted. A screaming flurry of black wings sent sheets of snow cascading to the ground, exposing the brilliant emerald branches underneath. Miles watched wordlessly as the dark, feathery cloud cleared the treetop and headed somewhere new. He signed his name and added the date.

Maya leaned over and kissed his cheek.

"What's that for?" Miles asked, surprised.

"Nothing. And everything," Maya said. "Are we ready to go now? Your mother is probably driving the kitchen staff crazy." They both laughed.

Miles took a deep breath, then exhaled. "Yep, I think so."

He started to return the clipboard and pen, then looked again to the sky. The flock was now a distant black speck against the intense blue.

"Make sure you indicate your relationship to the deceased," Marquez said.

"Of course," Miles said.

The blank line at the bottom of the page waited for him. He hesitated, rolling the pen between his right index finger and thumb.

Then, a crooked smile creased his face.

"Of course," he repeated.

Miles firmly gripped the pen and wrote:

"Son."

ABOUT THE AUTHOR

Tom Hernandez is a writer, public speaker, performer and communications professional. Born and raised in Joliet, Illinois, Tom has been writing personally and professionally since childhood. His writing explores the many complicated facets of life — marriage, family, relationships, identity, aging, parenting, faith, social justice and politics. He and his wife, Kellie have two adult daughters and welcomed their first grandchild in 2018. They live in Plainfield, Illinois.

www.tomhernandezbooks.com

Made in the USA
Columbia, SC
18 August 2019